I0817770

Human Maps

by

Andrew Hook

Human Maps
by Andrew Hook
ISBN: 978-1-908125-45-3

Publication Date: November 2016

This collection copyright © 2016 by Andrew Hook

Tetsudo Fan copyright 2013. First published in Rustblind & Silverbright (Eibonvale Press).
The Perfection of Symmetry copyright 2012. First published in Chiral Mad.
The Human Map copyright 2012. First published in Where Are We Going? (Eibonvale Press).
Blue Sky World copyright 2010. First published in Music For Another World (Mutation Press).
Bothersome copyright 2013. First published in Darkest Minds.
Vulvert copyright 2015. First published in Confingo #4.
Periscope copyright 2014. First published online at Perihelion SF.
Monster Girl copyright 2012. First published in The Monster Book For Girls (Exaggerated Press).
Beyond The Island Of The Dolls copyright 2013. First published in Postscripts to Darkness.
Rain From A Clear Blue Sky copyright 2013. First published in Black Static #33.
Cling copyright copyright 2010. First published in The View From Here #17
Wounder copyright 2011. First published in 13 (Morpheus Press).
The Quickening copyright 2012. First published in Shadows & Tall Trees #3.
Flytrap copyright 2014. First published in Interzone #253.
Black Lung copyright 2014. First published in Black Static #43.
On The Beach copyright 2011. First published in Unspoken Water #1.
Old Factory Memories copyright 2014. First published online at Axolotl.
Dizzy Land copyright 2011. First published in Black Static #26.
The Opaque District copyright 2014. First published in Horror Uncut (Gray Friar Press).
Things That Are Here Now, Things That Were There Then copyright 2012. First published in Dark Currents (NewCon Press).
Blood For Your Mother copyright 2015. First published in Black Static #48

All stories have been edited for this collection.

Cover Art by David Rix, copyright 2016

www.eibonvalepress.co.uk

This collection is dedicated to Clara and Nick Forster, whose wartime correspondence inspired the title story.

Acknowledgements and grateful thanks are due to the editors who previously published these stories. I am therefore indebted to Allen Ashley, Michael Bailey, Sam Bellotto Jr., Adam Bradley, Andy Cox, Terry Grimwood, Mark Harding, Ian Hunter, Tom Johnstone, Michael J Kannengieser, Michael Kelly, David Rix, Timothy Shearer, Ross Warren, Anthony Watson, Ian Whates, and the multiple editors at both Axolotl and Postscripts to Darkness magazines.

CONTENTS

Tetsudo Fan

Saturday morning Kazuo packed his camera and lunch into his rucksack and headed down to Tokyo Station. The day was bright. Sunshine bounced off the sides of glass buildings like the metallic sphere in a pinball machine. Kazuo's mother had waved as he left their apartment, and Kazuo had ducked his head as though he wasn't her target. At fifteen he considered that he was coming into his own as an individual. That morning his mother was the only shadow on his thoughts.

He rode the bus, his knees pressed close together, the bag on his lap. Other passengers were quiet. Two girls whispered together on the back seat, their voices no more than susurrations in the air. Some men clutched briefcases. Women held shopping bags that dangled from long straps over their shoulders. Kazuo took all this in, as though he were capturing it on film. One day, he thought, he might feel part of it, but currently despite his best efforts he remained an outsider.

At Tokyo Station he hurried to the Tōhoku Shinkansen line. He had many photos of the various 'bullet' trains in his collection, but he hadn't long been a tetsudo fan and there were always new pictures to be taken. Some of his friends collected stamps, others photographs of wildlife, some of them even collected girlfriends, but what Kazuo liked most about the trains were that whilst they had the permanence of stamps they weren't static, and in spite of their movement they were not as transitory as birds or girlfriends.

He laid his rucksack on a surprisingly empty bench and removed the camera. Checked the settings for light. Then sat and folded one leg over the other, waiting for the musical announcement of the train. He was expecting to catch one of the 200 series, the first type that had been introduced on the Tōhoku Shinkansen line in 1982. Whilst most had been withdrawn, some were still in operation as 10-car sets. Unlike the more modern N700 or E5 series the 200 series couldn't maintain speeds of 300km/h but still ran at an impressive 240km/h. Besides, Kazuo wasn't in it for the speed. There was a beauty to the design of all of the trains that spoke to something inside him. Something that favoured travel, exploration, excitement, and the thrill of the sounds of metal upon metal.

The earlier 200 series Shinkansen trains didn't have the shark nose of the 100 series, and they were lighter and more powerful than the 0 series. Kazuo wished he had been around to see those that were originally painted in ivory with green window and lower bodyside bands, but those still in existence had been revamped and refurbished, and he satisfied himself with sight of the white upper, dark-blue lower scheme with the wrap around cab windows.

Either way, they were sleek. Kazuo stood as one entered the station, slung the rucksack over a shoulder, and then bent at the knee to get his best shot.

His camera clicked repeatedly. He knew that if he flicked through all the images one after the other he would create the illusion of movement like an old-style flicker book. He could video the train, of course, but he wanted the static image. In some respects, the flicker photographs created a more staccato sense of movement than the real-life video image. For Kazuo, it was a more realistic movement.

Once the train left the station he returned to the bench and opened his rucksack. His mother had packed some *bocchan dango* together in a clear plastic box. Each of the types of dumpling, one coloured by red beans, another by eggs, and the third by green tea, were skewered together, three on a stick. There were five sticks in total. He placed the first in his mouth and pulled all three off simultaneously, the mix of flavours odd yet pleasant on his tongue.

After lunch Kazuo intended to catch one of the E4 series. These were double-decker cars, similarly painted to the 200 series although the nose dropped at the front as though diagonally sliced. As he chewed on the dumplings he imagined the kind of photograph that he wanted to take. Preferably a face front shot, then moving to one side to capture the length of the train. Some of the websites he frequented mentioned hotels with 'train-view' rooms where you could get a good view of the rails, trains, and stations in one shot. The rooms also afforded guests overhead views of trains that ordinarily could only be seen from the side. Yet Kazuo had no expectations of being able to frequent such places, just as some of his friends had fantasised about going to love hotels they remained just that: a fantasy.

The lid on his lunchbox popped back with a satisfying click. Kazuo replaced it in his rucksack and, camera in hand, made his way to another part of the station.

Light filtered through the building, reflected off the trains, illuminating the faces of pedestrians angelically. Suddenly for Kazuo all seemed right with the world, despite his overbearing mother. He was outside. He was with trains. There was a niche to be had and he squeezed inside it.

As he approached the platform an E4 series Shinkansen was ready for boarding. He would have to satisfy himself with photographs of it leaving the station rather than arriving, and whilst he always found something more exciting in an arrival he uncapped his camera and prepared his shot all the same.

Taking his first photo, a shadow distorted the light, and just for a moment he thought of his mother. Looking up he saw a man in casual dress, also with a camera, also pointed at the E4.

Kazuo stood. The man regarded him briefly. Then they both looked back at the train as pedestrians boarded.

"Two eight-car sets have been coupled together," the man said, his voice low. "That sixteen-car E4 series formation can carry a total of 1,634 seated passengers. It's the highest-capacity high-speed rail trainset in the world."

Kazuo nodded, unsure what to say.

The man looked at him again. Then raised the camera and took Kazuo's picture. "Always good to meet another tetsudo fan," he said.

Kazuo remained standing, dimly aware of his own camera held tight by his right hand.

"My name is Kunihiro," said the man, "I come here every Saturday and Wednesday when my wife is at her pottery class."

He looked at Kazuo expectantly.

"Kazuo," Kazuo said, at last. "My name is Kazuo."

Kunihiro nodded. "Someone young like yourself interested in the trains is important," he said. "After the E4 leaves, maybe I could take you somewhere."

Kazuo felt the aftertaste of the *bocchan dango* at the back of his throat, the green tea flavour over-riding the others.

"Ok," he said. Then he raised his camera and snapped the E4 in its static position.

The sun was still beating a ferocious rhythm as they left Tokyo Station. Early afternoon was bathed in stark light, like the difference between a digital photographic image and traditional film. Faces seemed pockmarked, teeth serrated. Smiles burnt themselves right into the corners of mouths. The blue and white of schoolgirl uniforms captured light and dark simultaneously.

Kunihiro beckoned a taxi and before Kazuo knew it they were travelling away from Tokyo Station and towards Akihabara.

The inside of the taxi felt like a vacuum, the unyielding light barely penetrating. Kazuo had the sudden thought of being in a cave. His rucksack sat between him and Kunihiro, an unspoken barrier. Briefly it crossed his mind to wonder what he was doing there, then Kunihiro answered that question for him.

"Have you heard of Shin Akiba Denki Tetsudou?"

Kazuo shook his head.

"Then you are in for a treat." Kunihiro steepled his fingers in front of his face. "It's a fictitious railroad company, also known as the New Akihabara Electric Railroad. You sure you haven't heard of the Little TGV Bar?"

Kazuo didn't know whether to feign knowledge. His lack of understanding concerned him, but in the end he simply shook his head again.

"Perhaps you are too young," mused Kunihiro. Then he unsteepled his fingers and turned to gaze outside the window.

Kazuo slipped one arm through the strap of his rucksack, anchored himself to the present. He wondered how old Kunihiro was. Surely in his early to mid-forties. His jet black hair should be speckled with grey streaks though Kazuo suspected it was dyed. He realised that Kunihiro was of similar age to his father.

When the taxi stopped, Kazuo thought about making an excuse to leave, but Kunihiro touched him by the elbow and together they looked up at the sign of the bar.

"This way," Kunihiro said.

Inside, the bar was decked out like the interior of a train. Young waitresses were dressed as railroad clerks, complete with caps. Their uniforms stopped above the knee although they weren't improper. Even so, Kazuo couldn't help but become transfixed by the sight of their long red and white striped socks. As they entered they were approached by one of the girls.

"How many passengers for today?"

"Two, please," said Kunihiro.

The waitress smiled. "You may have to share a table with others, is that ok? It will take an hour to reach your destination."

They were handed two train tickets and the waitress beckoned them to follow her down the aisle. Either side were seats as if on a train, memorabilia decorated the walls, somewhere out of Kazuo's sight he could hear a model train racing round a track, the familiar *shoo shoo* noise settling him.

As they made their way further into the restaurant the waitress called out 'two more passengers on board.' Kazuo glanced at Kunihiro to see if he was smiling, but his expression was fixed. So was his gaze, also at the socks of the girl leading them to their table.

"So," Kunihiro said, as they sat, "tell me about your interest in trains."

Kazuo recovered some of his composure. He explained how from an early age he had been interested in trains, from his first train set to his first journey. He omitted the fact that he had chosen trains over stamps, birds and girlfriends and he omitted the reason why. Kunihiro only appeared to be listening to half of what was said. His eyes looked around the room as though he were examining the scenery. The drinks on the menu carried railway related names. Kunihiro had ordered Hanzomon Line for himself and Ginza Line for Kazuo. Kazuo sipped his drink softly. He had refused food as he was still full of dumplings, and anyway he did not want to impose too much on Kunihiro's generosity, but the man had ordered *omuraisu* for himself, and when the omelette and rice arrived he had the waitress write the name of Takasaki Station on the side of his plate using tomato ketchup.

"Next Saturday," said Kunihiro, "I want to take a trip to the Hara Model Railway Museum. Will you accompany me?"

Kazuo found himself nodding. Today seemed a day for nods.

"Good," said Kunihiro. "We will meet at Tokyo Station at ten o'clock sharp."

With that, their encounter seemed to be concluded. Kunihiro dropped his head to his meal and Kazuo found himself rising and making his way back out of the train. As he left one of the girls caught his eye and beamed at him.

"Thank you for riding our train!"

Entering into the sunshine was like emerging from a tunnel.

During the week Kazuo found himself wondering about Kunihiro. It seemed he had found a kindred spirit, but the circumstances of travelling to the Hara Model Railway Museum troubled him. Whenever he had imagined a companion he had shyly considered it would be a tetsuko, a female railroad enthusiast. Sometimes whilst riding the trains he would look at the girls reading *Tetsuko no tabi*, a travel manga about a female manga artist with no particular interest in trains, who travelled the country by train with a travel-writer who is an enthusiast. That dissociation yet immersion appealed to him. Despite deciding to choose trains over girlfriends he knew it wasn't a real choice. Truth was, he had not yet met a girl who he could feel comfortable having a relationship with.

His mother was pleased with this. "You have no need to rush into anything, Kazuo," she might say, as she dampened the corner of a tissue and cleaned dried toothpaste from the side of his mouth. "Besides, whoever you find will have to match up to me."

Kazuo would nod, almost blush with embarrassment, and then flee to his bedroom with his railway magazines and the soothing hum of his Plarail model trainset.

Unlike the previous Saturday, rain fell in torrents when Kazuo awoke. The drumming of the rain had infiltrated his dreams as the hum of train tracks, and when he awoke he had an obscure feeling that he had been travelling.

In the kitchen he sidestepped his mother's questioning over his plans for the day. Shortly after nine he found himself on the bus, its wheels creating mini-tidal waves at the edges of the pavement as it winded its way towards Tokyo Station.

Kunihiro greeted him with a slight nod. Before Kazuo knew it they had taken the Tōyoko Line and then the underground Minatomirai Line to Yokohama Station, following which they made a short walk to the museum.

"A special treat," Kunihiro said.

Kazuo was well aware of the Hara Model Railway Museum. It had opened only the month before and housed an extensive display of model trains built and collected by the model railway enthusiast Nobutaro Hara. Even so, the museum could house only one sixth of his collection. As they walked around the exhibits Kazuo marvelled at the dedication.

Kunihiro also seemed obsessed. "Imagine," he said, "if something should happen to this collection. An earthquake, maybe. Imagine how the exhibits would fall apart, buckle under pressure, how these little figurines would fare in such a scenario."

"And yet," Kazuo intercepted, some of his shyness evaporating like the rain on the streets, "consider how during the Shinkansen's 45-year, 7 billion passenger history, there have been no passenger fatalities due to derailments or collisions."

Kunihiro tilted his head. "There is that," he said.

At the centre of the exhibit they paused for some time before 'Ichiban Tetsumo Park', a 310 square-metre diorama featuring model trains from all over the world.

"Imagine," Kunihiro said again, "that this landscape is the real world. We would be like Godzilla if we were to mount this display and crush it beneath our feet."

Kazuo looked at him, to see if he were joking, but Kunihiro just repeated 'like Godzilla', and he lifted each foot in turn, stamping the ground underneath him as if to emphasise his point.

"Godzilla," he said.

As they were leaving the museum Kunihiro's eye seemed to linger on a woman with a girl around Kazuo's age following in her wake.

"A *mamatetsu*," he said, and went over to speak to her.

Kazuo leant against the wall of the museum, hunger pangs affecting his stomach. He hadn't eaten all day, despite the dumplings in his rucksack. He had felt embarrassed to offer one to Kunihiro and therefore had eaten nothing himself. Equally, he didn't want to embarrass Kunihiro by having him pay for his food. As he mused over his position, he became aware of the girl standing beside him.

"I'm Neko," she said, extending a hand which was soft, cold, and limp to his touch. "Your father is talking to my mother."

Kazuo saw no reason to contradict her. In any event, words caught in his throat. Neko had a bobbed fringe haircut, which extended long at the sides and spiralled in two ponytails at the back. Her eyes were accentuated by black mascara, and her lips were highlighted with soft pale pink lipstick. When she smiled, something tugged within him.

"Are you *tetsuko*?" he asked.

She smiled again. "Sometimes. I have an interest, often I have to hide boredom. It's my mother's hobby. She still thinks of me as her little *kotetsu*. But, of course, I'm too old for that."

Kazuo noted calmly how the front of her blouse pushed forwards as she stood, one leg casually against the other. She wore a large pink bow at her neck, one that matched her smile.

"And you," she asked. "Are you tetsudo?"

Kazuo felt inexplicably challenged, as if she were mocking him. He shrugged off her attention and began walking towards Kunihiro. "Yes," he said, "yes, I'm tetsudo. It's what I am."

When Kazuo reached Kunihiro he saw he was talking animatedly with Neko's mother, yet his gaze kept sliding away to a corner of the room where a party of schoolgirls were congregating. Kazuo glanced at them himself, thought he recognised one, then realised Neko was at his side again, her eyes wide open with curiosity.

"Are you rude?" she asked.

Kazuo was taken aback. "Sorry?"

"I said, are you rude? I wouldn't have walked away from *you*."

But try as he might, Kazuo couldn't express his feelings.

"Come," Kunihiro touched his elbow. "It's time to go."

On the train back to Tokyo Station Kunihiro said, "There's something I want to show you."

Kazuo almost rolled his eyes. "The bar again?"

"No," Kunihiro said, "not the bar. Would you come to my apartment? It's just a short journey from the station."

Kazuo looked out of the window. It was no longer raining and the summer sun had dried the landscape. There wasn't a drop of water to be seen against any of the buildings, even in the areas that were shadowed.

He looked at his watch. "Only if it won't take long," he said.

Kunihiro smiled. "Of course. Just for a moment."

They completed the remainder of the journey in silence.

Entering Kunihiro's apartment Kazuo found himself looking out for his wife's attempts at pottery. Kazuo's mother had undertaken a similar creative course herself, and for a while their house had become littered with misshapen lumps of clay, before his father had finally suggested that they would make better use in the garden. But in Kunihiro's apartment there was no indication of his wife's hobby. Instead, there was much to illustrate that Kunihiro himself ruled the roost in his own home.

Railway memorabilia decorated the walls. Train tickets preserved behind glass. Uniforms on hangers. Pamphlets yellowing with age.

"My goal," said Kunihiro, "was to ride every line of every railway company in the country. Of course, we have approximately 160 different railway companies and the largest alone has over 20,000 kilometres of track, but I was sure it was possible. I used to colour in blank route maps to show where I'd been, though of course this has now moved onto the internet which automatically calculates the travelled distance just by entering the name of the railway line. For me, this takes the fun out of it, so I abandoned my challenge."

The entrance to the apartment was narrow. In the silence which followed Kunihiro's admission Kazuo could clearly hear his breathing.

"In here," said Kunihiro.

Kazuo followed him into a room crammed with a model trainset layout save for an approximate six foot by two foot gap in the middle of the floor. Stations, tiny people, trees, hedges, tunnels, barriers: the full set-up like a miniature yet still impressive centrepiece similar to the Ichiban Tetsumo Park at the Hara Museum.

"Lie there," Kunihiro said, pointing to the space in the floor. Kazuo looked at him expectantly, querulously.

"Lie there," Kunihiro repeated.

Kazuo became aware that intentionally or not Kunihiro was blocking the door.

"It's ok," he said. "There's just something I want to show you." Then he lifted Kazuo's rucksack from his shoulder. "Just in case," he said.

Kazuo felt himself carried as if by a dream over the tracks and into the centre of the room, tiptoeing through the display. Dropping first to his knees, he edged himself into position. It was only as he lay down that he noticed the flat-screen television face above him on the ceiling.

"Wait there," said Kunihiro.

Kazuo heard the flick of a switch and the trains which had previously been stationary came into life. Models of all sizes and descriptions began to circumnavigate the track. It was unclear from his position, but he estimated at least twenty trains began to run faster and faster, approaching his body from all angles then turning away, the noise in his head cumulative as the trains met in an arc and then sped tangentially in all directions.

The effect was soporific. The swish of the wheels on the track, the hum of the engines, the breeze that was created by their movement. Kazuo felt at home, probably for the first time in his life. A sanctuary was created within the cocoon of the tracks. Within the niche that was his world he had found another niche: a refuge within the whole.

It was then, just as he felt he might settle into sleep, that a film began to play on the television above his head.

It started innocuously enough. A young girl walked in and around a model railway set much as the one that surrounded him. She was wearing a schoolgirl uniform, although it was obvious to Kazuo that she was too old for school. Then she bent over one of the stations and he realised he could clearly see her white panties.

He tried to sit with a start, but a pressure seemed to hold him down, as though a centrifugal force from the trains that circulated him had pinned him to the floor.

The image changed. A woman in black PVC boots, tight pants, and a rubber top was gyrating over the model railway. She wore stockings, and Kazuo became open-mouthed as she extended a gloved finger to caress the top of one of the trains. The shot panned further back to reveal her high heels. Suddenly, without warning, she lifted a foot and stuck the point of the heel into the top of the train station.

Kazuo heard a gasp in the room, but couldn't turn his head from the screen. The girl raised her leg again, the camera angle affording a glimpse of her thighs, then she rammed her shoe onto one of the tiny plastic figures standing by the station. His body broke in two, one arm crushed sideways like an insect.

The camera remained focussed on her heels as she trampled across the set. Grassy hillocks were crumpled, carriages broken underfoot, each step marked with a sickening crunch and forced laughter. After a while the woman was joined by the schoolgirl and they set about decimating the diorama together, linking arms, with their hands around each other's waists. Kazuo was aghast yet consumed simultaneously. He remembered Neko at the museum, replaced the schoolgirl with her image. He remembered Kunihiro speaking of Godzilla crushing the exhibits. As the PVC-clad girl stood on a railway bridge at the exact moment a train crossed it, Kazuo closed his eyes and shivered deep inside his being. Not only was he home, he had found his heart.

The image ceased and the whirr of the trains came to a halt. In a daze, Kazuo finally managed to turn his head to one side where Kunihiro was standing, leaning against the wall, breathing hard, looking as if he were about to collapse.

Kazuo closed his eyes again. Replayed his memory. He realised he had made a jump from being *tetsudo* into adulthood. He pitied his friends who had chosen stamps and the arbitrary fluctuations of birds. They could never know the simple pleasure of a train.

The Perfection of Symmetry

Vermillion Chandler looked at her agent over her grilled-chicken salad and avocado. "Why that's great," she said. "That's really great."

She took small mouthfuls whilst Diana ran through a list of upcoming work, nodding appropriately. "I can do that. I can do that. I don't think I want to do that. You'll have to persuade me to do that! I can do that, yes, I can do that. Is that next Friday? Yes, I can do that."

It was all artifice. Vermillion knew Diana would have already confirmed appointments and her acquiescence was but shadowplay. Not that it mattered; she trusted Diana. They had worked together since Vermillion first started on the model circuit and had mutual respect. Many other girls were in worse positions and many wanted to be in her position. She was Diana's sole client.

She bit into a piece of avocado, taking it between her teeth before closing her mouth. Although they were in a secluded section of the restaurant, there was always someone with a camera wanting to make a buck through an indelicate photograph. Preserving her image preserved her image. And it was an image that needed to be preserved.

Diana smiled and said, "Well, that's it." She looked down at her own plate, which she hadn't started, then put her diary to one side and dug in.

The smell of hot juices running off the steak on her agent's plate made her stomach flip. She forked grilled-chicken into her mouth. It was excellent, but she missed the taste of red meat. Her dietician approved of red meat, though to Vermillion it was a slippery slope; like bacon to a vegetarian. Her figure—her entire body—was her fortune. She was twenty-two. It wouldn't last forever, and she needed to milk it for as long as she could.

Vermillion had been an ordinary child. Then, around the age of thirteen, her physiogamy kicked in like hot plastic poured into a showroom dummy mold. Her body perfected itself. Complete symmetry from head to toe.

"Who are you seeing, Vermillion?"

"No one, currently."

It was an ongoing joke. Vermillion's contract made it quite clear she couldn't have a partner for another couple of years. *Men fucked you up*, Diana said; and she had the lines on her face to prove it. Beneath the rhetorical question lay the veiled threat. Despite the joke, it was a serious business. Diana's income depended on Vermillion, which depended on her looks.

She smiled, rashly, her fork on the way to her mouth. A piece of avocado slipped back to the plate. Diana shrugged and whispered: "It'll be ok. It really will be ok."

After the swimsuit photo-shoot, Vermillion made her excuses and journeyed home. She preferred to take the wheel; there was power in the physicality and she didn't want everything done for her. At red traffic lights, she watched the faces of male pedestrians. She hadn't kissed a boy since she was eighteen: wayward, disinterested, unassuming—she had tasted fame and it bored her. But her pushy mother's death had changed everything. Money came her way out of the trust fund and she became used to a certain standard of living, and appreciative of the effort it took to maintain it. There was little point in spoiling herself while filling the bank. Other pleasures would come later.

Even so: men walked in suits that fit snug, Hawaiian-shorted guys looked like grown-up kids, others were less attractive but were no doubt great in other ways. Despite her looks, Vermillion knew the adage of beauty being skin deep was a truism. She had known enough models—male and female—to be sure that looks didn't matter in relationships.

Back in her apartment, she drank coconut water and cooked an egg-white omelette on whole-wheat toast. She was twenty floors up. Wide floor-length windows fronted her view of the city. Sun poured naturally out of the sky, creating a paler blue near its edges. She pressed her hands against the glass and leaned forward, buoyed by her reflection doing the same. She looked down at the street far below: the cars like coloured boxes in a square slider game, the roads cubing the buildings in a way that you couldn't tell from the street. Vermillion allowed herself a smile. She enjoyed the height. She craved the perspective.

A loud bang shook the glass. She gasped: her mouth forming a perfect O. The seagull disappeared as quickly as it had arrived, leaving a feather glued to the other side of the window by a drop of blood.

Vermillion realized she was shaking. Her reflection did the same. The feather waved like a fascinator before the breeze took hold and it slowly descended toward the dead bird on the street.

Vermillion slept fitfully. In a dream, she heard a sound under the floorboards and eased them apart to find a deep well beneath. There was someone at the bottom. She squinted, couldn't quite make out a figure as the cylindrical brick walls tapered to a point. Almost-words drifted upward. She woke from the dream with a shivering sensation that someone had been behind her, about to push.

By the breakfast bar, she juiced beets, spinach, ginger, carrots, orange and celery while waiting for an egg to boil. The egg itself contained symmetry, she realized through the noise of the food processor. She remembered someone at High School telling her they had once cracked open an egg and a half-formed chick had fallen into the frying pan.

It was only after breakfast and after her bath that she stood in front of her full-length mirror.

Before she became symmetrical, before all of this happened, she had asked the typical child's question: *Mirror, mirror on the wall, who is the fairest of them all?* She was just an ordinary little girl, although an uncle, on her father's side, once said: *Do you realize you have the most beautiful face?* In Tianna's bedroom after school, they lay on the duvet and held mirrors up to their half-faces. Tianna's nose was slightly crooked. With the mirror vertical, her nose bent in on itself. Vermillion's nose looked like Vermillion's nose. There was no distortion. The only time she looked any different was within the travelling funfairs' Hall of Mirrors.

She allowed her silk dressing gown to slip off her shoulders. Naked, she was perfect; clothes only served to rumple her image. The symmetry of her body had long been documented, as had the correlation between symmetry and beauty. A combination hardwired into the public consciousness. Many models had fairly symmetrical faces, a handful had *perfectly* symmetrical faces. Vermillion's symmetry was such that she didn't need to wear make-up. More importantly, where Vermillion differed was that she had the perfectly symmetrical body to match.

From her smallest toe through to her knee caps through to her buttocks through to her vertebrae, through to her shoulder blades, through to her breasts, through to her cheekbones, eyes, ears, nose and forehead: Vermillion was perfect. The symmetry only ended inside her body, where the organs lay in the usual lopsided places. But no one was interested in her interior; it was the exterior which brought the money.

She smiled at her reflection, which smiled back. The smile mirrored itself, left to right and right to left, just as it mirrored in front of her. Sometimes she wondered if she were simply one-sided, if her right half was a hologrammatic representation of her left. But this was not so. The match was complete down to the tiny light-brown birthmark on her right hip and the tiny light-brown birthmark on her left hip.

Not only was her visage perfectly symmetrical, she also had the optimum ratio between her mouth, eyes, chin and forehead.

For the avoidance of any doubt, and to accentuate the fact, Vermillion opened her mouth and said: "I'm perfect."

"Hold it, hold it, hold it right there."

Vermillion held her gaze as the camera flash fluctuated like strobe lighting. Behind her, a white backdrop caught the glare. Diana stood beside Gee, the French cameraman working for *La Femme Actuelle*. In the pit of Vermillion's stomach, a knot of hunger gnawed at her concentration. She tried to push it aside, but remembered the dead chick when cooking that morning's egg, and in turn, the seagull slamming into the window. She had called the building's maintenance to ask them to remove the blood smear. Nevertheless, like the ache in her gut for a tuna sandwich, the remembrance of the smear was dogging her day.

In truth, she had forgotten about it until she had dressed and was ready to leave the building. With one hand on her door handle, she glanced back into her orderly and well-maintained apartment and a shaft of sunlight had shone through the smear like stained-glass.

"Smile. Smile. Smile!"

The camera clicked.

Diana ran a hand through her hair; like a lion's mane, it held shape while remaining wild. Vermillion had the sudden urge to touch her own hair, its Louise Brooks bob being the best design to accentuate her looks. Hair was one thing she couldn't control. Nail growth, another. A charge of irritation ran through her at the duration of the shoot. Gee had enough shots. She stuck to her pose as though frozen. Then her hunger got the better of her and she threw the soft teddy bear she had been holding to the floor and stormed off the set.

"Wait. Wait! Miss Vermillion. I just need a few more. Wait."

The walk to the dressing room was a short one, but Diana made it there first.

"What do you think you're doing?"

"I'm hungry. I can't concentrate."

"You're not in love?"

She laughed. "No! What makes you say that?"

"Because love is the only thing that will destroy your beauty."

Vermillion held up her hand. "Woah. We're talking about you, not me."

Silence.

Then: "You're right. You're right. Of course. Gee's taken enough photos. I'm starved, too. Let's go get something to eat."

The restaurant manager welcomed them both with open arms, managing to acknowledge the pair of them while not taking his gaze from Vermillion.

"Come, come. Your usual table is free. The quail. You will have the quail, yes?"

They sat. Vermillion pressed her knees together. She watched as Diana folded and unfolded her napkin, the edges never quite returning to their pre-folded state. Vermillion had been described once as having perfect symmetry like a paper chain person, as though she had been folded in half and cut from only one side. She had liked the metaphor until she thought of a linked procession of such figures. She had been petulant in her early days as a model. She wanted to believe she was unique.

The quail arrived: lightly grilled, sprinkled with lemon juice and served on a bed of arugula. A spaghetti side dish with sausage and peas in a mild cream sauce accompanied the meal. Vermillion knew she would eat it all. That she *should* eat it all. Diana sometimes disapproved of the restaurant, though she could never fault Vermillion's determination to remain true to her cause. Slips in diet were regulated; slips in diet were necessary.

Sometimes, when both of them felt like it, Diana would regale Vermillion of her own time in the trade, when models weren't expected to be perfect and discrepancies could be airbrushed without legal scrutiny.

"Sometimes I look at those magazine covers and I don't see the person I was," Diana said. "I mean, I always expected my pigmentation to be whitened, whether through make-up or digitally, but when I saw how far they had zoomed in on my eyelashes and lined them up like soldiers, I couldn't quite believe it!"

Vermillion nodded. The quail tasted good. Juice from the cooked bird mixed with a little blood, creating a pale red lake on the plate. She detected a slight pepperiness that sat on her tongue and pinpricked it; smooth, it felt like it was absorbed into her mouth, rather than consumed.

"Your mother was against all that, of course. But she had a secret weapon; she had you."

Diana touched her lips with her napkin. "I mean, it's not as though she led the lawsuits against airbrushing, but she was verbal. She paved the way for you, but you know that. And it was the right thing. It enabled true beauty to come to the fore, once again, even if some people didn't like it and were pushed aside."

"You're not much like her," Diana said. "Well, apart from your determination. She lived her life through you. That much was obvious. Again, you know this."

The arugula had a slight bite to it, which matched the pepper in the sauce. She rolled one of the leaves around with her tongue and for a moment it stuck to the roof of her mouth. She sipped lemon water and dislodged it.

"Vermillion?"

"Yes?"

"Are you happy? Would you say that you're happy?"

"Yes, Diana. I would say that I'm happy."

Even after the meal, the ache in her stomach didn't go away.

⊙

If there was much store to be had in the meaning of dreams, it wasn't a philosophy that Vermillion bought into. Some believed they were a subconscious reflection of the conscious, like an alternate world with just as much a right to exist as the real world. Some would say that the dream world and the real world were reversed, that *reality* was the dream, and the *dream* was real. Vermillion awoke from a dream where a man had clutched himself between her legs, his hand moving forward and backward, as if he were immediately about to push.

She wrote her name in the steam that formed on the glass in the shower.

In her dressing room mirror—there was no mirror in the bathroom, no chance for her image to be distorted through condensation—she stood full-length naked.

It was rare that she let go to admiration. Despite the scientifically proven assertion of her being, she was constantly looking for the blemish, for the shock that would cause the image to shatter. It was there; she knew it. One day it would fly in on the wings of age and her uniqueness would be destroyed. She wouldn't be able to continue her career as an almost-perfect model like the other girls. The only option would be to retire and to... what, see the world? But she had already seen the world. She had seen the world on a red carpet. Once that carpet was pulled away, the protection she was afforded would be gone. Magazines would no longer need to court her, they would send their paparazzi to photograph her diminishing looks in ill-fitting swimsuits, she would be plied with drink and captured falling out of taxis with the white V of her knickers on display, she would be the trophy-fuck of the first man who charmed her. She would be nothing—one hundred percent zero—without her body.

Regarding herself in the mirror, she saw that the fall from grace had yet to happen. There was no more or less to her than yesterday. Another day of smiling and posing; another day of loneliness surrounded by people.

They hadn't cleaned the blood on the window. She woke with that surety.

She strode into the living room, her silk pyjamas swishing like whispers. It was still dark. She hadn't checked her clock, but judging from the lights in the surrounding buildings, it couldn't have been much after two in the morning. Night-owls played cards, drank, made love: with her hands pushed against the windowpane, she envisaged it all—a whole world waiting to be discovered, a world that would be soiled once she found it.

She pressed the right side of her face to the glass, closed her eyes, and imagined the window giving way, of falling toward the ground like a wingless angel, a cloth in a final flutter over a table. She saw her body, broken to pieces on the ground: her limbs at wrong angles, her face twisted, a pavement Picasso. Residue of a dream seeped out of her and pooled around her body. Then she snapped her head away from the window and out of the reverie. Goosebumps ran uniformly along her arms and at the base of her neck.

Vermillion walked through the darkness of her apartment, lit only by the moon and the soft hues of the building's security lights. Her cast shadow bent against the side of a table.

Her shadow wasn't symmetrical.

It came down to light. That was it. It all depended on the light.

When she moved, her shadow lifted itself from the sofa, ran along the floor, and then up the side of the doorway. Half of it fell through the open door, the rest hung against the jamb. She raised an arm to her head; the shadow did likewise in a jerk as it ran over the light switch. Vermillion held her breath.

Was this what it was like to be normal?

In her dressing room, she stood before the mirror with the light off. Her outline was indistinct, the edges blurred. She looked like a smear, as though viewing her reflection through condensation or through the blood on a windowpane.

When she disrobed and turned on the light, she knew something was different.

She watched her reflection watching her, scanning her cheekbones, shoulders, arms, hands, legs, hands, knees, hands, hands, hands.

Her arms hung at her sides, the thumbs of her hands facing inwards, almost touching her thighs. Within the reflection, her thumbs were opposed; they faced outward, *away* from her body. The palms were hidden, her arms as they should be, but the fingers… the fingers were all wrong.

Symmetrically, she was still perfect, yet the mirror lied.

The mirror *was* lying.

She raised her hands to the glass and pushed them flat against the cool surface. Her middle finger touched her middle finger, but her index finger touched her ring finger, and her thumb touched her pinkie.

Breath caught in her throat as she stepped back. She watched her reflection for some time before snapping the light off. The sudden absence of light created blackness and dizziness, as though she were falling—falling into a well littered with broken eggshells and bloody feathers.

And within that blackness she twisted. She rushed toward the mirror. Glass shattered and her reflection held her, vertically, in a position that remained until she was found the next morning. Almost in a pose.

The Human Map

MYANMAR

The tiger bounded out of the surf, chasing white horses. Spume frothed its mouth, but surely it was I who was mad. The sun pressed against my neck like a cigarette, as though someone was sat in the undergrowth with a mirror, scorching me as I used to scorch ants.

Paw marks larger than my own hands held together as one fist made patterns in the wet sand. Nearby, a much larger circular shape, a hollow, as though the sand had been blown out by a vacuum cleaner in reverse. Or a helicopter, I realised. But bigger. Much bigger.

The tiger wasn't interested in me. It's black and orange colours flashed across my retina, playing with my senses. After a while it was gone, mildly bedraggled. I watched it move further along the beach until it entered the jungle. Once lost, my fear increased. There was nothing, no one, other than me on the beach. I sat alone.

So I stood. My black jeans had long faded to grey, my t-shirt likewise. My Converse hugged my feet, as comfortable as slippers, as comforting as reality. I lifted one trouser leg and saw I wore no socks. Touching my forehead grains of sand aggravated the pain. I ran my tongue around my lips. Water. I needed water. I ran my tongue around my lips again. I craved water.

Slowly, I moved away from the beach and into the shade. Palms hung heavy with coconuts. Husks littered the floor. I picked one up, the rough coarse hair prickling my skin. Repeatedly I threw it against tree trunks until it cracked and I managed to craft a drink through the fragile slit. The coconut water sweet, too sweet, the edges of the husk itself were bitter. I slept.

Waking at night the jungle sounds mingled with memories in my dreams.

Angeline sat opposite me, her feet dipping into a washing up bowl, the water moving between her toes, fluid. I remembered the scene. We had only recently bought the property in Norwich and had gone walking one summer's day to see how far we could go. It had been eight miles to Wroxham and eight miles back again. She showed me her blisters, bubbling the skin like black plague boils, but clear. I washed her feet that day, with the sound of monkeys in the trees outside the terraced house reverberating through the brick, stimulating my ears.

I shook my head.

Dreams fell out. My eyes were encrusted with sleep, with sand. I threw the coconut again and it split in half. Even then, my teeth could barely peel off enough of the thin white flesh to eat.

It took me a few more hours to seriously consider what I was doing, by which time morning was up and there was a dark-skinned boy on the beach. He was sitting within the circular hole, holding a stick. I watched as he pointed the stick towards the sky. Laughed.

Fearing for my sanity, my life, I wandered out of the jungle's edge and onto the sand. Danced on the hot surface. The boy noticed, stood, and ran into the undergrowth.

Maybe only one of us could remain on the beach at any one time.

I stood where he had sat. The circle was over fifty feet in diameter. The sand within had become glass. A polished surface. My soles blistered. I couldn't remember.

I reached into my pockets. No money, no phone, no keys. The boy returned with an older male wearing a red and blue striped sarong.

I pointed at myself, and said in the international language: "English."

I didn't understand the language that returned to me. Guttural sounds, hard consonants. The boy touched my arm, smiled. I followed them back into the jungle. My stomach growling like the tiger.

A few days later I understood where I was. Myanmar, once Burma. On the Andaman Sea. On the Tanintharyi peninsular.

Burma.

Be Undressed Ready My Angel.

MALAYA

"Sssh."

I began to open my eyes but fingers pressed them down. Soft fingers. I wondered if they were Angeline's.

Then I heard chattering in a foreign language and realised that despite the dreams I was yet to be home.

Sounds assailed me. As though becoming aware of one sound had been a portal to hearing others. The squeaky wheels of bicycles, the shouts and grunts of market traders, the swish of rain, the steady stream of water running from a tap. And then smells: durian, mangosteen, rambutan, lychee, pineapple, banana. I knew each as it came to me, somehow. The warm chilli scent of the body lying next to me, the smell of the heat and the rain. And then the fingers were removed from my eyelids, but I still kept them closed. Afraid to open them, to see what I would see.

So Angeline returned to my vision: we had argued. Her face, her lips, were pursed to a point directed on a scuff mark on the black tiles in our kitchen. Tension, frustration, fermented inside me, was contained.

I opened my eyes. I lay on a bamboo mat, spread on the mattress of a four poster bed. Green wooden shutters were pulled against the windows. The walls were bare, plastered over the brick: cool and smooth. Upside-down I watched the smiling face of the woman who had closed my eyes. She stood, walked backwards, descended wooden steps in the corner of the room. When I sat, my head swam. There was a television in the corner, switched off.

I stood, held the banister. Moved stiffly towards the window. Gripping the ridges of the shutters I pulled them open.

Outside was a town. Two roadways heavy with traffic. Cars and motorbikes interweaved, intertwined. Entire families rode each bike. In the distance, the sun was descending, a bright orb melting the scene as one, imbuing the atmosphere with a golden glow. I breathed in the hot air, moisture from the humidity as thick as milkshake.

Before I heard the footsteps on the stairs I saw two things. One: all traffic was heading out of the city. Two: a series of wooden buildings had been flattened in a circle fifty foot in diameter. Smoke rose, blackened the updraft like an American Indian signal. But this wasn't America. This was elsewhere.

A hand touched my shoulder. The girl again. She gesticulated to an older man, his hand on the top of the banister, who hauled himself into the room. Pale cream shorts offset his dark legs where feet fed into sandals. His shirt was multi-coloured, patterned with random images. Although not random, designed.

"I am Mr Pong."

His English was faltering. Within twenty minutes I had established that nothing electrical was working. Televisions, phones, the internet: everything was down.

"Since when?" I asked.

"Since you came," he said.

I was about to ask more, but then I wasn't there.

Malaya.

My Ardent Lips Await Your Arrival.

ITALY

The headache is severe. Like a migraine. Yet I've never had a migraine, so how do I know? Lights flash.

I'm beginning to realise that all my experiences are condensed. I stand behind Angeline as she peels potatoes and wrap my arms around her stomach, kiss her hair which smells of papaya. She moves backwards slowly, into me. We merge.

This time when I open my eyes I'm surrounded by people jabbering and pointing. They keep their distance, and if my math is anything to go by the nearest isn't closer than twenty-five feet. I'm circled. I'm at the centre of a circle. The ground under my back is blackened. I can feel the heat of it through my t-shirt like a scorch mark. There's a taste in my mouth that I don't recognise, something metallic. But not blood, maybe old money. Something alien.

I squint as the sun is reflected from the wing mirror of a scooter that pulls up at the edge of the circle, and for a moment the people are reduced to nuclear shadows.

When I look at my arms I see track marks, ley lines that terminate elsewhere on my body. I touch my forehead and a hard ridge of dried blood runs full circle, as though I've been lobotomised in some b-horror movie.

The chattering increases as I move into a sitting position. I recognise some of the language. That is, I recognise sounds, not words. Most of the men are wearing white vests. The younger women have cut-off denim shorts, t-shirts. Older women wear flowered garments. Older men have hats. As I scan the crowd I see mobile phones pointed towards me, yet something's wrong, no one can get a picture.

I know where I am. This is Italy. It comes to me in a flash and in another flash I'm gone. I'm getting closer, I'm moving close to you Angeline.

Italy.

I Trust And Love You.

FRANCE

I begin to expect it when it happens. I begin to know what to expect.

Angeline is sitting on a chair with her feet on the table. *Konnichiwa* a voice says. She repeats it: "Konnichiwa". *Arigato* the voice says. "Arigato" she repeats.

From somewhere I hear my voice say, "Alligator".

She grimaces and throws something at me which disappears before it reaches my head.

Japanese segues into French. After a brief exchange of words, French segues into English.

"Are you okay?"

I want to nod but my head hurts. Knowledge is a burden.

My tongue is thick in my head. Have I already spoken? "Where am I?" This is me.

"Limousin."

Something comes to me about the number of farmers and suicides in this region.

"I'm being used," I say.

My vision which was previously blurred now comes into view. An elderly gentleman with map-relief wrinkles on his face bends over me. He extends a hand and I rise.

"*Je ne comprends pas.*"

I look beyond him to his tractor parked in the distance. He is a wheat farmer and we're standing in a crop circle.

"I'm trying to get back to England," I say.

"England." He nods. "*Angleterre.*"

"Oui," I say, thankful for my schoolboy French. He taps my shoulder, and almost in a hug we begin to move forwards one step at a time.

He takes me to the tractor, and I sit with my back against one of its large wheels. Cradled. In the cab he removes bread, cheese, ham. We sit together, staring at the crop circle, whilst he halves the bread with a penknife and slices cheese.

"Did you see it?" I ask.

He shakes his head.

For a moment I wonder if he thinks I did this.

For a moment I wonder *if* I did this.

Memories are fragmentary.

How I've sat, my jeans have ridden up my legs. Twin circles of dried blood surround my ankles. I've been dissected, bisected.

The bread could be manna. The cheese is a bonus. The ham sits on my tongue and stifles it.

"There's a girl," I say. "There's someone I'm trying to return to."

It doesn't seem like he understands. From a pocket he pulls out a silver bottle of water. Only it isn't water, and when it burns my tongue I find myself slipping away, being pulled back into that other space. That other space I cannot remember. Unlike France. France which I do remember.

France.

Friendship Remains And Never Can End.

HOLLAND

I'm getting closer. Angeline is pulling me back, rewinding me, like a thread from a ball of string. Only there's a cat, a tiger, also following the string. When she tugs, it jumps.

She's pulling me back through her memories.

We stand on Southwold Pier. The light is incredible here. Just an hour's drive and life is transformed. To our right, fishermen cast their lines, buckets only full of water at their feet. To our left a couple embrace. I glimpse a tongue. Angeline is taking photographs of seaside binoculars. When she shows me later the twin lenses are eyes, the ridge between them a nose, their metal casing a head. "They look like robots," she says. And I have to agree: they do.

I wake in water. It's dark. Pitch black with no moon and cold. I pull myself out of the dyke, realise my breaths are heavy. They're too heavy. Asthmatic. I reach in my pockets for my inhaler then remember where I am. No. Not remember where I am, but remember what I am.

Or maybe, not even that.

I pause, regulate my breathing, return to normal.

I lay on my back looking up at the stars until morning comes.

As the sun shifts behind me, illuminating greenery, I find my shadow waffled: I'm sitting in a square of light. I turn and look behind me, see the windmill, sun burning squares through its slats.

It's broken. Inside smells of urine and I step around broken glass. Take the steps one at a time to the top. From a tiny window I obtain a good view. The dyke is fresh, the earth dark and moist around it, and the line of the dyke takes a circular route until it returns to itself. Once again, a cut in the earth, as though made in a flat plain of pastry with a cookie-cutter. In the distance I see a road. Cyclists. I limp out of the windmill without a hope of reaching them, and that's true because then there's that tug again and I'm out of here. I'm out of Holland.

Holland.

Hope Our Love Lasts And Never Dies.

WALES

It's only here where I begin to understand.

I understand that I've overshot.

They pick me up from the field and take me to the nearest pub. There's more sheep than them. I'm rural.

"What's happened to you then?"

For some reason they're suspicious. And I sense that it's more than me. There's other.

"I don't know," I say, needing to be honest, needing to find a voice.

They mutter amongst themselves.

I look around the pub. There's a television in the corner which isn't on. There's no light within the refrigerator behind the bar, and no flashing lights on the fruit machine. It's dark in here. On the surface of the bar and on the tables are candle residues. It's been a while.

"How did you get here?"

I shake my head. This could be dangerous.

"I've been travelling," I risk.

One of the men snorts and before I know it I'm being strong-armed out of the pub, two of them either side of me. I'm marched down a rough street with grass growing in the middle of it, like a green Mohican. A couple of basic shops and several small houses flank the road. Children watch me. At the end of the road is a police station. In any other situation this would be photographic. I remember Angeline and her camera.

"Come here," she says. And then, "No, there."

I walk backwards and forwards whilst the shutter clicks.

Later we pull close and she holds the camera out in front of her at arm's length, the lens facing us. That photograph is the first to grace the mantelpiece in our new Norwich home. I can see it now, superimposed over this Welsh scene. One of the older boys is running behind me, trying to kick my legs out from underneath me. I wonder if I'm going to be beaten up. Certainly friendship has faltered the closer I've gotten to home.

Home.

Hope Or My Extinction.

Inside the tiny police station there are no police officers so they put me behind a desk and leave the room. Two of them watch the door at the back, and two of them watch the door at the front. But I'm not going anywhere.

At least, not that way.

Then I do leave. I leave Wales behind.

Wales.

With A Love Eternal, Sweetheart.

NORWICH

I'm back. The experiments are over. For now.

Angeline's sitting on the corner of the bed with a smile on her face. I'm not sure if the smile is for me or even if the smile is in the here and now.

I stand in the doorway. Rings encircle my body, as though I've entered a fancy dress competition as a lemur. Tears fall in big droplets from my eyes. I see myself reflected in them as they hit the wooden floor.

"You're back," she says.

Behind her through the window I finally see the craft, for the first and last time. It rotates like a Catherine Wheel on its side. All silver and beautiful.

"Back?" I say, "I never went away."

I don't tell her that I'm aware what Norwich stands for.

But then she turns and I see something isn't quite right.

She's transparent.

It's transparent.

Parts of me unfold like a paper animal. A reverse origami.

What are we, after all, but refractions of light interpreted by our brains? What is time, but a linear cheat? Where are we going, other than to places we have already been.

They're inside my mind, extracting the human from maps of my memories, my DNA, my future, my love.

I know where I am.

Amount of Responsive Extraterrestrial Abductees: 51.

Unlocking secrets of the human race viewed from above.

Blue Sky World

They called it The Tear. Not simply because it was a rift between time and space, nor because of its shape—like the gap between badly drawn curtains—but because of the emotion it carried through to us after it had wrung its way open. An emotion that would linger, long after the experience was squeezed dry.

Sometime before this was known I found Sidonie by the roadside. Hitchhikers were rare, and she didn't have her thumb out, but you could tell she was expectant all the same. It was a country road, the ploughed fields stretching away either side towards a grey horizon, with all the soft brown of corrugated cardboard. Her clothes were odd, mismatched, as though stolen from a washing line. Her hands were hidden within her sleeves. Her skirt could have wrapped around her twice. Her stance was skinny, her face was full. You could see the life there as though it had only just been invented. Unlike the colour of the fields, her skin was a richer, living brown. I pulled to the side of the road, careful to avoid the ditch which I knew would be hidden amongst the greenery. She ran round to the driver's side of the car and stuck her head through the windowspace.

"Where are you going?"

"Into town. About five miles from here. Want a lift?"

"Of course."

She ran around the front of the car, briefly touching the bonnet to steady herself, before wrenching open the passenger door and sliding inside. When she slammed the door closed, water droplets flecked off the glass.

"On the run?"

"Pardon?"

"Nothing." I put the car into first gear, gently manoeuvred away from the verge, and gradually increased speed as I passed through to four, pondering the lack of houses on either side of the road.

"What are you doing here?"

"Nothing. I just arrived."

We continued in silence. I could tell she didn't know where we were headed; the name of the town or the route we were taking. I took several diversions in the hope of continuing the conversation, even if there wasn't much of it. Within the confines of the car she closed in on herself, like a butterfly reverting to the chrysalis. Yet she was confident, her eyes darting across the scenery, taking it all in like a first-time tourist.

I turned on the radio to fill the car with noise. I located a station that specialised in movie songs, my preference being words which linked to scenes which linked to films which bled into life. A girl was singing in French, a slight refrain with simple guitar accompaniment. Her voice was uncluttered, direct. I thought it must be Michèle Torr or Bardot. Then I realised my hitchhiker was singing along, initially mouthing the words before hitting them full flow, a voice as pure as Bardot's; *purer* than Bardot's. There was such joy and sincerity through the physical act of singing that I felt tears forming in my eyes, and I shook my head as if to flick them away like the car door droplets onto grass.

The song ended. The announcer confirmed it was Bardot, from the movie *Vie Privée*, directed in 1962 by Louis Malle. The piece was called *Sidonie*.

"Hey, that's my name," newly christened Sidonie said beside me.

"You know the song?"

Her brow creased. "I don't think so?"

"You knew the words?"

"I pick up on these things."

"You know French?"

"Un peu."

"A little." I translated absentmindedly. Then I veered off the road, bumped down a track used by tractors, and onto the field. I reached over and switched off the radio before the ignition.

She didn't ask me what I was doing.

"Can you remember it?" I said.

"I think so."

"Sing."

I closed my eyes as she repeated the song. Her voice was delicate, perfectly pronouncing each individual word, and although I couldn't understand the meaning I was totally wrapped in the moment. It was like the purest poetry: words that you read which connect deep inside without needing to understand them. Her voice had that quality, that insistence. When she finished I opened my eyes and a film of water temporarily obscured my vision.

I wanted to ask her if she had ever sung professionally, but the words hung back in my larynx. It was the pause before the ending of a performance, where everything holds still until the first clap, before the thunder of applause. It seemed to last longer than was necessary, until I finally felt able to clear my throat.

"Bravo."

She smiled. "It was good?"

"It was stunning."

I thought she blushed, but as the sun was setting and swathing the fields in red I might have been mistaken.

"Where I come from, I am only a beginner."

I didn't ask where that was. I felt like kissing her, but instead I turned on the engine and as we pulled back onto the road, mud embedded deep into the tyre tracks, I asked her if she had planned somewhere to spend the night.

She didn't. But I did.

I took her to see Xavier two weeks later. We had prepared at my apartment with its recording studio and soundproofed walls. No one could hear us, morning or night. I watched his face as the CD player lasered out the music, teasing out the sound. When it finished and he stopped gripping the armrests of his leather chair I swear I could see his fingerprints imprinted on the material.

Although I had now been frequently exposed to Sidonie's voice, there remained that fluid moment where life rolled and revealed itself before either of us could speak.

I wasn't sure whether Xavier chose his words and spoke carefully, or whether he enunciated them that way because he could do little else.

"That was incredible."

Sidonie smiled. Gave a little curtsy, which was girlish yet powerful. Her short blonde hair caught the sunlight and glowed. The weather had been looking up recently.

"We have to do something with this."

"Don't we."

I conferred with him whilst Sidonie glanced around the room, read the sideways spines of the books on the shelves, and gazed curiously at the signed photographs of the songstresses on the walls.

"Are we the first?" He asked me. "Surely she has sung before?"

I told him what little I knew. She was amnesiac or an autistic savant or both.

He asked me and I told him that the sex had been great.

"Her memory is fresh," I added. "Play her anything and she can repeat it. Note perfect. No, more than that. You heard her. More than perfect."

"More than perfect." He repeated the words as though he needed to. "This is true. It annoys me when people say they give 110% because it's not possible. But she does, she gives more than one hundred percent."

I clasped his hand. "So you'll distribute it, right?"

He smiled. "I have a choice?"

We drove back to my apartment. I had kept her hidden away those two weeks. Phone off, doors locked. Once I glimpsed my girlfriend, Angelica, through the window as I crossed from bathroom to bedroom. She looked like she had slept in her car. When Sidonie came to find me, Angelica threw a stone at the glass, instantly cracking it to shape a spider's web. Through the shards I watched her leave.

Whenever I asked Sidonie about her past she simply smiled and said it was a secret. I wondered whether it was secret even to herself.

But there were documents to be drawn, papers to be signed. I pressed for a surname but none was forthcoming. Xavier had intimated we would need one for the contract. So I took her along the road I had found her, the ploughed fields having since been seeded, the clouds no longer an encompassing grey but individual and edged in silver.

"Do you remember this?"

I stopped the car close to where I had picked her up.

"Of course."

"Where did you come from?"

She shrugged. As if the question had no meaning. Or if she couldn't divulge the answer.

We continued along the road. The fields merged into woodland, the woodland into heath. Ten miles further the army research base appeared on my left. Sidonie moved towards me like a shadow bent away from approaching light.

"Here," she whispered. "I think it was here."

I couldn't stop. Two sentries manned the entrance. In any event, there was nothing to see. The base was a long way back from the road, down a driveway which once housed a stately home. So we continued, and it was only after we had gone a few hundred yards that I realised via my rear view mirror that the sky above the base was blue.

◌

She sat on the edge of my bed, naked, her legs dangling, not quite touching the floor.

"Are there more of you?" I asked. Not knowing if I wanted an answer.

"As many as in this world," she said.

"Are there more of you here?"

She looked up. Her irises were the colour of a marble that I once smashed in half as a child, returning eyes to my teddy bear by affixing with superglue the pale twist of green.

"I don't know."

Again, I found myself asking a question wary of the answer.

"Will they be looking for you?"

She sighed. "I expect so."

I held my head in my hands. The contract, the papers, the CD.

"Sing to me."

Her song was unlike any other I had heard. The words were part of the music itself, like opera yet more intense because it clung instantly to your heart without any build-up or introductory emotion. It was a keening; not as a lament but as an expression of joy, uncontaminated by the slurries and disappointments of this world. I closed my eyes and the lids glowed as the song progressed, tiny rainbows striated my view. When the song finished and I reopened my eyes I could see it wasn't her who shone, but the sun streaming in through the windowpane.

I stood and pressed myself against the wall-length glass, unselfconscious of my nudity. The clouds had minimised, no longer had a touch of grey but were brilliant white. And the spaces in-between were impossibly blue. I felt warmth on my body, for the first time in an age. I struggled to remember how long it might have been.

I turned back to Sidonie, half-expecting her to cry. But she was only smiling, her white teeth matching the colour of the clouds.

"My secret," she said.

I sat beside her, stroked her face. She held my hand, put my fingertips inside her mouth. It was then that I realised her voice was a sonic orgasm, sustained and intense, yet untainted by the sometime rigidity of sex. I craved her. I needed more.

Xavier telephoned. I had unblocked his number. "The CD," he said. "It won't be enough. We need a concert. She must do a concert before we release the recording."

He was right. In the two weeks I had been trying to capture her voice I knew the recorded version was a poor imitation. A fantastic vocal, unheard of, it was true. But a copy nonetheless.

"Bring her back to my office."

I flipped closed my mobile. Sidonie's brow contained that frown, but she wasn't upset only puzzled; just like an animal when something unknown shades its knowledge.

"I'm not sure what to do," I said.

"Do what's for the best."

"For who?"

I paused.

"If there are more," I said. "Will they have your talent?"

She laughed and the sound caught my breath like a fragment of song.

"I haven't much talent," she said.

o

I checked all my windows, locked all the doors.

Sidonie regarded me through the cracked pane as I waved from the driveway. Her body splintered myriadly, unaccountably. I gunned the accelerator and gravel arced upwards, sparkled like gemstones in the glare of the sun.

I collected Xavier from his office. Further down the road, opposite the pub, two young men, their t-shirts crenulated by muscles like relief lines on a map, got in the back.

We drove off the highway. Parked in the metal structure of a threshing barn. I got out and pulled at a bale, extracted an almost unbreakable sliver of straw, bent it round my fingers as the men told us their story.

"Some kind of research," one of them said, "into the structure of time and space. We opened something and it stayed open and wouldn't close." He shook his head with his inability to describe it.

The other took over. "It's not like the movies. It's not like the books. There are no demons. There's nothing to attack. It's just beautiful. Just incredibly beautiful."

He blanched at his words. Unaccustomed on his lips.

"Imagine a world," Xavier said later, "where everything could be as we chose. A blue sky world. Blue sky thinking. You know that expression? It's corporate nonsense, a type of brainstorming which acknowledges no limits. Whatever the army have been doing up there, they've tapped into a world where this is the norm, the reality. They've split open the sky and let purity in; like a beam of religious light."

"You believe that?"

He shrugged. "You know how many times I've played that CD?"

I felt fear then.

"Do you think it's closed?" There was a tremor in my voice.

"How could I know? What are you thinking?"

"I'm thinking if it's closed then they'll want to hush it up."

"And if it's still open."

"Then they can't hush it up."

We drove past the base. There were still sentries outside. I wondered how many others our young men had spoken to. I knew Xavier had slept with one of them. In the barn I had tried not to think which. There weren't just singers, they had said, but musicians, conductors, lyricists, composers. If our world had made technological advances, theirs had proceeded in the arts. There was no comparison. They had taken the right path.

As before, the sky over the base was a deep marine blue. An open sky that I guessed nothing could close.

I took Xavier back to my house. Sidonie smiled when she saw him, she hadn't had much contact with people. He was gentle, held her hand and kissed it out of reverence; there was no sexual spark between them. We entered the studio and Sidonie sang. There was no point adding musical accompaniment, it would only detract.

Her voice soared and dipped, weaved back on itself. I thought of Sirens, but dismissed them because here there was no intent. Just unadulterated musicality. A surge of emotion. She interspersed her own songs with material I had written and the difference was obvious. Yet she could sing the phonebook and we'd be weeping. She finished with *Sidonie*, the briefest of songs, a language familiar yet unfamiliar. Xavier fell to his knees.

Afterwards, wiping our eyes with the backs of our hands, the three of us hugged, a mutual moment of appreciation.

We didn't know what else to do.

It went beyond us. Beyond borders and governments. Was given a name. The Tear.

Yet like all artistic perfection that comes into this world it was tainted: assimilated, backlashed, thrown back. With only a residue remaining.

Unlike Sidonie. Our unknown pleasure. Because we kept Sidonie's secret. We kept Sidonie secret.

Bothersome

When I wake I remember that I used to be. Someone.

My joints ache. I slowly sit up on the bed and reach out one hand, feel my way around the walls. The paper is embossed, like some alien kind of Braille. My eyes are open but the patterns, shapes, are unfamiliar. The room isn't quite how it was meant to be.

But me. I have this recollection. Sunshine on my face. My brother, teasing me because I'm a girl. Throw the ball. *Catch*. Drop. Throw the ball. *Catch*. Drop.

That was how it used to be.

More than that. In the lab. Looking for something amongst the rats. The mole rats. Looking for the secret of longevity.

I never used to be much trouble.

◎

I kick at something with my feet. As I bend down my back gives way and I stay like that.

Some time later I bend further. Pick up a circular bowl containing yellow liquid. As I swirl it first one way then the other I recall the conundrum about which way the water spirals down a plughole on the other side of the world.

There weren't many female scientists when I was young. I used to urge women to do things. *Remember: a horse threw itself under Emily Wilding Davison for you.* It usually got a laugh, not always the right kind. I made a play of being different, but it was a cocoon, a shield behind which the real me could function without being seen.

Like a controlled experiment.

As I return the bowl to the floor it tips and stains the carpet. Where are the windows in here?

Some time later I wake up and remember I used to be someone.

But I never used to be much trouble. Kept myself to myself. Hands in my pockets.

I watch my brother run over the dunes. Sand flicks up from his heels. *See where it lands!* There's broken glass hidden there. My foot on a stool in hospital. Grains and blood and pale white skin. It'll be alright. There's a hand on my shoulder. I know I'll be alright.

It's all a matter of knowing where to look.

I bump into something else, feel my way around it. A large rectangular object made with wood, standing vertical. There's a key which I turn and when I reach into the interior it's like fumbling inside the stomach of a knitted animal.

There's a musty smell too. This object hasn't been opened for a while.

I try to climb inside, but there isn't enough footspace. Tugging on something my balance falters and I tip and it tips and I'm lying on the floor and the object has enclosed me with an almighty bang like the closing lid of a coffin.

◎

When I wake up I remember.

I visited a zoo inhabited by balloon animals.

At the centre of the earth, I once postulated, was a giant mole.

No one ever knew if they should take me seriously.

I knew that they shouldn't. Except when I was being serious.

I laboured the point. Just to be obstinate. I often found it was at the wrong angles where truth was to be found. Just like the fountain of youth. But no one understood that either. Unlike me, who knew it was sometimes in the fifth bottle of a six-pack of Evian water on the third row of the seventh aisle in the supermarket.

Once, I drank from it.

If I listen very carefully I can hear voices through the floorboards. Which floor am I on? Top or bottom I suppose it doesn't really matter. There's a murmur, nothing distinct. No words. I crave words. I suddenly and absolutely crave words. I need to be fed.

Running my hands over my legs I feel shocked at how old and waxy the skin is. Pulling at the sides of my thighs near the bone it almost peels away, like unfurling a sail. When did this happen?

I continue feeling my way around the room, avoiding the wooden rectangular object which has been returned to its place.

Why aren't there any mirrors?

I could ask, but I really don't want to bother anyone. I don't want to be of much bother.

My hair is brittle. Both on my head and between my legs. There's my brother again, laughing. A semi-circle of his friends stand around me and I'm too young to understand. I don't understand why I'm naked. Nothing happens, they just look like all boys like to look and then he tells me the facts of life and I'm dumbfounded and know immediately that I want to know more I don't want to experience more I just want to know more I want to know all the secrets of the universe and suddenly I realise I have the power to know what ticks inside each and every one of us.

I've aged. Somehow, when I wasn't looking, I've aged. And my work is far from complete.

૦

When I wake I realise I am already awake.

I'm standing beside another rectangular wooden object, flat against one wall. I'm gripping something with my arthritic fingers that feels like round porcelain, but however much I try to twist the knob it's only my hand that moves. When I push it doesn't budge. There's the potential of movement there, for sure. I must be doing it wrong.

On the other side of this object I know someone is holding their breath. A shadow moves in the light underneath the door, recedes. Everything is receding.

I find my way into a corner. It's all angles, all the wrong angles. I won't find the answers here.

Is there a clock somewhere?

I invented something and I no longer know what it is.

They laughed, eventually, at the mole in the middle of the earth. It tugged at my mind until I realised that *hot mole centre* was an anagram of *the molten core*. They didn't believe it was coincidence, thought they had been tricked. But the trick was only with the words that played out in my mind and made me see that there are signs in everything.

I reach out and touch things with my hands because I can't trust my eyes to see.

There's pain in my stomach. When did I last eat? Again, I move, knock into the headboard. Full circle then, full square. I'm lost.

I lie across the bed sideways and it hurts. My body can't be at every angle anymore.

My memories are a dandelion clock. Each time I take breath, some are blown further away. Yet. Yet. There are always those which cling resolutely. Those that haunt.

૭

I wake a younger self. Watch me as I kiss the shoulder of the sleeping man beside me, his musculature firm and exciting under my lips. I sit up, run a hand through my short hair, stand, dress. Pull on socks whilst balancing on alternate legs. Without holding onto anything. I'm an acrobat. I urinate almost clear. Clean my teeth. Open the refrigerator and bathe in the yellow light, cast a shadow of myself on the floor behind. The milk is cold. It courses down my throat. I remember my mother telling me never to drink from the bottle. I always did.

I see myself take my keys, slowly close the door to the apartment. Descend the interior lift of the building to the underground carpark. My car makes an electronic sound as I press on the fob and suddenly I'm inside and feeling the engine hum around me as I manoeuvre this steel machine between the concrete pillars and merge into daylight as though being absorbed.

There's laughter in the office which continues as I enter. I'm well-liked. They can take the nonsense about my balloon zoos and hot mole centres because they know it's a side effect of being a genius. A quirk. My intellect is in the motorbike, my peccadilloes are in the side car. It balances me. Keeps everything at one level, one angle.

I am the bent paperclip that isn't meant to be straightened.

I watch closely as I lean over a test tube. I am about to discover something important. Really, very, important.

o

I make another circuit of the room. What's happening here? There's something I can't grasp. I know what it is, but my brain won't allow me to remember. What I mean is that I know I know the answer. But I don't *know* the answer.

I could knock on the walls, on the wooden objects, yet I just don't want to be a trouble to anyone.

It's only after I've been to the toilet in one of the corners of the room and thrown a towel over the top of it that I see the metal circular bowl beside the bed.

When I sleep someone enters. I'm not sure if that's physically or spiritually, although what I am certain of is that they're standing over me and saying something like she's got lost in her own room again.

And if that was the case. If that *was* the case. Then why don't they leave the door open?

I remember a red pencil. HB. Stem hexagonal rather than circular. With a point of graphite at one end and an eraser at the other. I journey along the pencil. From the graphite making marks on paper at one end of the journey to the eraser removing them at the other.

What was it Stan Laurel said? *You can take a horse to water but a pencil must be led.* It always made me smile. *He* always made me smile. Despite, no because of, the inaccuracies.

What is memory after all: a collection of misremembered inconsistencies?

Sometimes when I throw the ball I catch it. And sometimes when the ball is thrown to me I catch it too.

I make another circuit of the room. The space where I had squatted before is clean and smells of something sharp. Like lemons. When was the last time I ate? Why are there no windows in this room? When was the last time I drank? In which location can be found the fountain of youth?

Sometimes it's in a puddle, under a motorway bridge. Sometimes in the saliva of a cat. Sometimes bubbled as dew in a field of freshly cut grass. Then again it's the hot tap rather than the cold. Then again at the bottom of the wishing well, carrying a coppery taste from all the coins. Sometimes it's in your own urine. Sometimes someone else's. What does it mean to be young anyway? When the memories are yet to be uncovered rather than remembered. Where do you draw the line? When do you erase it?

I know they come for me when I'm asleep. I wake in fresh clothes, my stomach doesn't feel empty, my lips aren't parched. But I miss the words, the conversation. *She's a daft old bugger.* Even that can be enough. It all depends on the intonation. On how things are said.

Mustn't grumble. This is my mother now. *Mustn't grumble.*

I morph into her. Wake up and find that I've become her. With add-ons and other technological advances. With other memories. Following a line that runs all the way from the past to way into the future.

Did I have a child?

Yes, because…

I get off the bed and kick the metal bowl into touch but this time it's empty.

Where did that handsome man go whose shoulder I kissed as I got out of bed?

Where did the girl go who got out of bed?

Where did the girl go whose brother nipped her as she lay sleeping?

Where did the girl go who heard her father whisper *I love you* as the blankets were tightened around her small frame.

Where did the girl go who pushed her way out through her mother's bloody thighs?

Where did the girl go who formed out of sperm and egg?

Where was the girl before any of this happened?

As I say, where did the girl go?

The mole rats were resistant to cancer.

My knickers are wet. I've soiled myself. I wander round and around the room, searching for a way out. I've become lost in my own room.

There's some kind of fabric obscuring the wall. When I pull against it light glares as though someone is shining a torch in my eyes. As though I have my face pressed up close against the sun. I tug on the fabric again. Shut out that light. Why aren't there any windows in this room?

Later in the day I see Gregory sitting on a chair however when I talk to him he doesn't answer and later I realise that the chair can't even be in this room.

Well, that must be something else then.

There was once more than this. Memory flickers true and false. Do those words really mean anything? As a scientist, how much did I discover or how much did I just uncover? There appear to be more questions now than ever before. Someone must have brought in a cup of tea but it's too cold, too milky and much too sweet to contain the fountain of youth. Even so, when I drink it there's a reaction inside me and my face contorts and I realise that I'm smiling.

Something's just beyond my grasp.

Something big is just waiting to be discovered.

When I wake and realise that I used to be someone, the shape of the bedclothes frame a porthole. I peer through it and see Earth receding, like a kicked football heading over a neighbour's fence.

Well, the cat's among the pigeons now. What are they going to do with me?

Is it possible, as an astronaut, to feel both agoraphobic and claustrophobic simultaneously?

I reach out for the glass of water beside the bed.

Here we go. Again.

Vulvert

She said she came from Indiana but studied in New York which is why her voice carried a nasal twang. I didn't care where she was from, only that she was there, sitting on the sofa with me, her legs dangling across mine as though I'd grown extra appendages. Later, we giggled that I had.

It was a season of surprises and calamities. The Ferris Wheel collapsed at the close of the August bank holiday. Revellers had already shuffled through the main gates, and the barkers had their backs to the giant structure. Eyewitnesses reported a resounding tear, as if the wheel were an eye shedding the death of the sky, then the back supports gave and the wheel jolted off the platform, rolled either a few feet or half a mile depending on who you believed, and fell into the adjoining cornfield intent on creating a crop circle.

I hadn't been to the fairground, but I could see the structures with their striped awnings and faux-glamour from my garret window. At that time I was renting the top floor of a building that an eccentric landowner had intended to resemble a castle. Funds for the structure must have dwindled, so more of the idea remained rather than the actuality. Since then, its idyllic countryside location had been swallowed by the city and if it hadn't been granted listed building status it would have been demolished to make way for the cloned houses which surrounded it.

The cries had drawn me to the window. By then the Ferris Wheel was lying in the field, it's lights still flashing like a UFO landing signal. For a moment I indeed thought that *they* had returned, even if the *they* were in my imagination. The crowd were caught between gazing and fleeing, the suddenness of the collapse belying the suggestion that anything could happen.

They weren't sure if it was over or just beginning. From my window I could see more clearly that it was over; but then again, it *was* only just beginning.

Out of the confusion she came.

◎

Say that again.

Vulvert.

And again.

Vulvert. What is this?

I smiled. It's velvet. You've transformed it with your accent.

She looked up, doe eyed. *Are you mocking me?*

I shook my head. Of course not. But from now on I'm going to call you Velvet.

Then she shook her head. *Not Velvet,* she said. *Vulvert.*

◎

Truth was there was more to like with Velvet than her pronunciation of velvet, yet I loved the way the word slid off her tongue, like a girl who'd climbed a tree and was trying to edge herself down without catching her skirt on the branches behind her. I was also drawn to the sonic association with vulva; and it seemed a natural progression from velvet to vulvert to vulva, just as the graze of my fingertips across both of the words evoked similar sensations. Not only due to our budding relationship did those words become symbiotic, interchangeable; but I felt there had always been those connections and only through Velvet had I been able to link them.

I worked as a linguist, so such associations held an allure which might not have been evident to a bricklayer or a comedian or an astrophysicist or even a gynaecologist. I blame my initial love for sounds from the phonic electronic toy my niece played with in her second year. I was thirteen and babysitting and bored. She sat transfixed by the television whilst I pressed the *F* and *K* on the keyboard in quick succession. *FfK. FfK.* My aunt slapped me across the back of the head when she caught me, stumbling through the door with my uncle, my niece long in bed and the toy remaining an auditory distraction.

When I told Velvet I was a linguist the conversation went something like this.

I see. Are you a cunning linguist?

We had been together for less than a week. The funfair had moved on and the debris dispersed. Everyone who had attended the fair seemed to own a little piece of it. Velvet had shown me a green light bulb, its filament intact.

All the others were smashed, she said, holding it up, ironically, to the light.

The bulb was a bright soft green, reminding me of the spines of some of the Penguin Classics on my bookshelf. At the base of the bulb the glass was clearer and at an angle almost impossible to achieve you could glance upwards and spy the filament. I took it from her and held the upper part of the bulb in the palm of my hand. It fit perfectly. Although I then wondered if it were the lower part of the bulb. Like everything, it all depended on positioning.

I had glimpsed Velvet from my garret window, as the sirens threw blue glazes on the brickwork of the cloned houses and the crowd had begun to properly disperse. She was alone. That much was clear. I remember thinking that she resembled a stone in the river, with the detritus of other life passing by and around her whilst she maintained her own pace. She wasn't completely stationary, but her movements seemed deliberate to the point of obstinacy. It was as though the damaged fairground were a magnet, pulling her back towards it, just as she strove to leave. I fantasised about running down the twisting stairwell to the street yet knew by the time I did so she would have vanished, so instead I watched her until she turned the corner at the end of the row of houses and disappeared without any help from me.

Online dictionaries with their pronunciation guides also fuelled my word-obsessed imagination. As children my parents would have flicked through books either white-crisp or yellow-faded to seek out definitions, their teen eyes flickering and their thin lips smirking at the rude words sat as though commonplace with their erudite contemporaries. Whilst for me it was the Internet with the clipped tones of a male or female voice intoning those words at the click of a button.

As I remember it now, a female pronounced the rude words which related to male body parts and a male voice did likewise with the female. But this might be a quirk of memory. What was a surety was that velvet wouldn't have been pronounced as *vulvert* even if I had listened to such an innocuous word.

I would open several windows at a time, preparing them with words to be pronounced in succession. In my mind this disembodied intonation, disjointed as I clicked each in turn, produced an eroticism lacking from simple pornography.

Kiss. My. Cunt.

I. Want. Your. Cock. Please.

In hindsight, these were innocent games. Quite unlike those which Velvet was to play with me.

You had to move quite some distance from the cloned houses to find any shops of interest. Even negotiating the labyrinthine streets was a task that sometimes confounded. Inevitably tradesmen would call at the *Castle* to ask for directions simply because the individual building was more approachable than the rows of similarity. The property itself wasn't officially the *Castle* of course, although the residents—mostly students, mostly studious—called it that, both out of affection for the architecture but also out of kinship with the Kafka novel. For us, it did seem that we were isolated in a village and that everyone was striving to connect with us. Although in truth, that glamorisation only worked from our perspective; the suburbanites no doubt wished that we didn't blot their landscape.

I had been flicking through second-hand CDs when I saw her again, the jewel cases click-clacking like high heels on a pavement. She stood opposite, head down, her long black hair parted down the middle with a pale pink strip of skin dividing the two sections of her head similar to the way the medial longitudinal fissure divides the two cerebral hemispheres in the brain. The pink strip had obviously caught the sun, reminding me of another simile: the thin strip of excrement retained within the body of a prawn, albeit with the colours reversed.

My own brain sent signals to my nerves which I couldn't quite understand. I was caught in a typical fight or flight scenario, and flight would have been so much easier.

If you're not buying that I'll have it, she said.

I looked down, almost uncomprehending, then realised I was holding a Sonic Youth CD, *Washing Machine.* Her accent tickled parts of me that only existed in that moment.

Take it, I said, my mouth swollen with happiness.

She smiled, insouciantly.

Thanks.

She walked up to the counter and paid. I gathered my wits and timed my exit from the shop to coincide with hers. Holding the door open I said I saw you at the funfair. After the wheel collapsed.

Did you?

Her expression was unreadable which meant unreadable was her expression.

Yes.

Words fell out of my mouth like stones into the body of a sleeping wolf, dropped by a goat armed with needle and thread. And as I awoke I became the wolf, consumed by a raging thirst.

Somehow, out of that, we shared a packet of crisps over a wooden trestle table speckled with the bleached white residues of bird mess, our fingers clasped around the necks of beer bottles and then eventually around each other.

ᴑ

When she looked around my garret apartment she spun and spun as though she were the farmer's daughter in Rumpelstiltskin whereas in retrospect it was *her* name that required guessing.

This is so cool.

I wondered how many words we had appropriated from Americans due to the upsurge of access to Stateside television over the past twenty years.

It's like, history, *or something.*

I caught her as she fell backwards into my arms, breathless at the audacity of her certainty that I would be there. Reality buckled against the romanticism of the moment, the give in my arms strengthened by my belief. We stumbled backwards until I steadied myself and falling onto the bed my spine jarred at an angle I would recollect for years to come.

Oh! Her exclamation a popped balloon.

This was when she reached into the pocket of her cardigan and pulled out the green light bulb. I was reminded of Katherine Mansfield's short story, *Feuille d'album,* where the potential suitor hands over an object he claims the Mademoiselle he has been observing has dropped: an egg.

All the others were smashed.

She held it up, to the sunrays spotlighting her through the window.

But see. It's intact.

Over those beers our lives had assumed the roles of exchange students. I had been dissected. When she laughed her eyes were containers of universes, some yet to be born. Her teeth were whiter than mine, which corroborated her story. She was on a gap year that had extended to two years. It had been a while since she was in New York and even longer than she had been in Indiana. Yet she hadn't lost her accent and wondered if it were possible to do so.

I told her it wasn't impossible, but that it would come through training rather than assimilation. Even then, linguists were sceptical as to whether an accent could truly be lost in everyday speech, although Charlize Theron and Anthony La Paglia were good examples of actors who had lost their native sounds and developed American accents without needing to think about it.

She placed the light bulb on the windowsill and sat on the bed. *Tell me more.*

You have to focus not only on the vowel sounds, of which of course there are five, but also the vocalic sounds of which there are twelve. You would need to identify an example accent to imitate. To listen and repeat. You would have to focus on the way you use your mouth, teeth and tongue to form the vowel and consonant sounds, modifying intonation and stress patterns and changing your rhythm.

She laughed. A bird caught in a net. *I'm not smart enough for that.*

I found myself silent, running a hand back and forth over the curvature of my right ear. I knew opening my mouth wouldn't ease the words coming out and so I reverted to gazing at her in the land where time stood still, until she breached the gap and leant into my personal space. Eyes wide open. We kissed.

When I was eleven I hung my coat on a peg outside the school classroom. The corded strap of my sports bag slipped out of my fingers and fell to the floor. I bent to retrieve it and when I straightened a girl stood there whose name I can no longer remember and her lips brushed against my cheek.

At fourteen I was pushed into the arms of a heavily made-up nineteen year old who used to sit on a street sign close to the Comprehensive waiting for a boyfriend who never arrived. My friends had laid a bet that she wouldn't kiss me, something I only understood years later. Her lipstick tactile on the surprised O of my mouth I wiped my forearm against my lips and removed it much quicker than I wish I'd done several seconds later.

Solitary kisses had peppered my life ever since.

Velvet I kissed twice.

And then a third time.

Vulvert.

I lay back on my bed, watching her inspect my wardrobe.

She had pulled out my velvet smoking jacket. I had never worn it, but sometimes whims had to be satisfied.

Is this vulvert?

Say that again.

Vulvert.

And again.

Vulvert. What is this?

It's *velvet* I said. You've transformed the word with your accent.

Call me *Vulvert* she said.

I laughed. It sounds like *vulva.*

She smiled. *Are you a cunning linguist?*

ʘ

Making love was awkward and Velvet knew it.

Afterwards she pulled the thin sheet back over her body, her hair damp and resting on her shoulders like seaweed over rock.

She leant on one elbow and pushed her index finger into the side of her mouth, then stiffened it and jerked it out. *Pop!*

Pop she repeated, like an actress overjoyed to get a speaking part.

Pop?

Your cherry. She inserted the finger again. *Pop!*

I felt myself blush. Was it that obvious. I should have said.

She laughed. *You don't have a cherry. I do.*

She laughed again. *Actually, I don't suppose there's such a term for a guy losing his virginity. But it'll do. You should know that, being a linguist and all.*

It was a season of surprises and calamities. All I could hear was the tear as the Ferris Wheel broke away from its mooring.

Velvet?

Yes?

But there was nothing I wanted to say.

ʘ

Summer segued into Autumn. Velvet called it Fall.

We saw each other frequently. I was happiest when we were sitting on my sofa, entwined, her legs over mine.

Then one day, like a boy's voice might transform as it enters manhood, Velvet's voice broke.

She stopped mid-sentence.

Oops.

Hindsight brings its own brand of wisdom. I remembered watching my mother count fifty pounds in fifty pence coins she had accumulated in the shop, all ready for banking. The first time she counted she came to forty-nine pounds and fifty pence. On the second count it was fifty-pounds and fifty pence. On the third count it was actually fifty one pounds, and only on the fourth count did she make fifty pounds exactly.

Finally, she said.

I sat up. How is it likely to be exactly fifty pounds just because you expect it to be?

Because I *knew* it was fifty pounds, she answered. And smiled.

The exact word in Velvet's sentence, spoken in an inescapable Lancashire accent, is unimportant. Even if it was my name. No longer was she a castle in a city of cloned houses. All the affectation—all the affection—was gone.

"I'll get my coat," she said.

It was only after she left that I realised she had taken my smoking jacket.

Sometimes *they* are only in our imagination.

Vulvert had looked at me once and said *no more guesses* even though I had no knowledge we had been playing a game.

A shark's brain bears a startling resemblance to a vagina.

My life has since been abbreviated.

Periscope

In the future all the Chinese were speaking perfect English in American accents. Despite the fact that American English *became* perfect English, little else appeared to have changed.

Dr Swe Swe Win popped the answer into the air tube transfer system, then ran a hand through his thick black hair. He glanced over to the window, where darkness had fallen slowly as though a black blind being pulled downwards over the view. Looking out he couldn't see *out*. The building was surrounded by the night: ambushed. Or, that was how it felt. Especially when working alone. It reminded him of the days when Aung San Suu Kyi's League for Democracy party had been suppressed. Sometimes it felt that night had fallen during the day.

He shuddered and decided against concentrating on his task. It was too late to think straight and the road from the complex could be dangerous at this hour. There was no longer a threat from bandits, but all animals were as attracted to lights as the humble moth. He had narrowly avoided a rhinoceros once, and didn't care to encounter one again.

All the doors were electronic, detecting the tiny sensors in his fingertips as he approached them and opening on cue. He moved effortlessly through the building, his soft shoes almost polishing the floor as he walked. His eyes were tired. He removed his glasses, rubbed his index fingers against his eyelids, and when he reopened his eyes tiny lights glittered his view of the white-painted walls.

He wondered what they would think of the message. It wasn't his role to interpret—and even if he wanted to, there would be no sense in it. Others were employed to detect repetitions and patterns. His job was simply to operate the machine.

The answers it gave were numerous, often conflicted. But it *gave* answers, that was the thing. It was the only machine that could.

Dr Swe Swe Win walked through the final door which—sensing the building was now empty—employed its security system in absentia. The night was humid. It felt as though a cloak had been thrown over him: one that had been seeped in animal musk and warm moisture. He detected his own body odour, masked by the air-conditioning within the building, given full reign now he was outside. The air was alive with insects and the loud *ki-wao* call of a male peafowl continued into the night.

Security lights illuminated the car park and his solitary vehicle. During the journey home he passed small shops set back from the roadside: corrugated metal sheets forming a shell from within which wooden tables held all manner of foodstuffs. He held back from grabbing something quick, decided to wait until he arrived home. Despite living alone, he liked taking the time and effort to make a good meal. On occasion, when Hlaing came to visit, she would compliment him on his culinary skills and gorge herself.

Sometimes, when he ate with her, he wondered if they were already in the future.

Other times—when her hand reached out to clasp his in a moment of passion—he wondered if they were already in the past.

***

His house was large for the District. It was raised on concrete pillars to avoid the monsoon floods. The surrounding land had been owned by his parents. He had inherited it and knocked down their humble home, added to the property as he rose through the ranks. Now it was spacious and light, expensive but not ostentatious. He didn't know what those in the surrounding villages thought of it, and didn't much care. The machine—if nothing else—had told him the future was changeable, and it was important to hold onto things whilst you had the chance.

He parked and entered the property. Headed straight for the kitchen and threw the ingredients together for *mohinga*: a fish soup made with chickpea flour, garlic, onions, lemongrass, banana tree stem, ginger fish paste and catfish served with rice vermicelli. It was breakfast food but it *felt* like breakfast at this time of the night, and he would save some for when morning came so as not to waste the surplus.

There were no messages on his answering service from Hlaing, so he switched on the television and watched the world at war. When that failed to amuse, he channel-hopped through a variety of cut-price reality and game shows and finally turned the screen black and stared at his reflection staring back.

When he had first devised the machine—completely by accident, he hadn't failed to admit that—tests had been extensively made on his vision, sanity, and peripheral mental health. Following confirmation that his discovery was genuine, the money began to flood in. Offers to develop the machine were thick and fast, and whilst many attempts were made to copy it they couldn't work without the integral ingredient: himself. The machine was copyrighted with *Dr Swe Swe Win* named as one of the components. Eventually, he had accepted the offer made by the League for Democracy and the competition backed off. The ruling party held respect—and respect authenticated the machine. And by association, authenticated himself.

It was exactly the kind of luck which had led him to meet Hlaing. And from then onwards enabled them to engage in their relationship.

She had discovered him in the staff canteen, eating boiled eggs dipped in fish sauce and chilli. Sitting next to him, her thigh length skirt exposed her soft brown skin. This was the first thing he noticed. The scars from the cigarette burns. He admired her audacity, her lack of shame. The fact that she was able to work within the complex indicated that the torture was in the past. He offered her an egg and she reciprocated with a fried fish cake. Her accompanying smile as white as a cigarette. Not that she smoked.

One evening she caught his arm as he was leaving the building. Her voice carried soft low tones into the forest which absorbed them quietly.

"Dr Swe Swe Win, they say you can predict the future."

He shrugged. "Prediction is for others. I can simply see the future."

"Isn't that the same thing?"

"Unfortunately not." He pulled out a photograph from inside his jacket pocket. The one he always used to explain his situation simply and explicitly. "Look at this." He passed the photograph to her. It was black and white, depicted a curving piece of silver-looking metal. On the curve, white light indicated the reflection of a flash.

As she held it he noticed her fingernails were bitten to the quick.

"What is it?"

"Not yet," he said. "Do you see it?"

She shrugged. "Yes, I see it. But what is it?"

He took the photograph from her hand, turned it around so that she might view it from all angles. She kept shaking her head. "You can see it," he said, "but you cannot predict what it is. You cannot see it for what it is. This is a close-up of one section of a household water tap. But you aren't given enough to be able to recognise it. You might be able to guess at what it is. But you might also guess at a lot of things that it isn't. You can see it, yet you don't know it. This is what the periscope gives me: the ability to see the future but not to understand it. I am unable to place it in context. That job is for others, although whether they are successful or not I am unable to tell. Again, I don't see enough of their work to enable me to predict it."

She nodded slowly. He was unsure whether she understood.

"And it is only you," she continued, "who can see it?"

"Currently only me," he confirmed.

She smiled suddenly. He felt the floor slipping away. "I just wondered," she said. "There are rumours about you."

"Rumours?"

"Not here. Outside."

He started to walk towards the exit, then realised she meant the rumours came from outside; not that she wanted to talk to him outside. But then she followed and she continued following all the way to his car, to his home, to his table, to his bed.

"Can you ask it anything?"

He shook his head. "I can only receive."

"If you could ask it anything. What would you ask?"

He sat up. The bedsheet fell from his body, exposed him to the waist. He leant forwards. She saw how his spine pushed against his skin and she ran a finger from top to bottom. Then back again.

He shuddered.

The question was a frequent one. He changed his answer each time, depending on who he was with. On occasion, he would reply that he would ask when there would be world peace. Sometimes he said he would discover the date and means of his death. Other times, whether he would have children. He alternated between the universal and the personal, between the serious and the humorous. With Hlaing he wanted to answer: *I would ask whether there is a future for us in the future.* But the very nature of the question contained a doubt that they might have a future together. So instead he said: "I would ask whether I will succeed in giving Hlaing an orgasm."

She laughed and punched his arm: friendly, yet not without vigour. "There are other ways to discover this," she said. "Try again."

Her laughter always concealed a question, just as her smile always held an answer.

ဝ

He awoke alone. He could smell the traces of the *mohinga* in the air, rotated by the air-conditioning, and wondered how long he had slept. Daylight forced its way through the metal blinds covering the window: almost buckling them, and throwing horizontal shadows on the opposite wall. Hlaing hadn't responded to his telephone calls after he had eaten his meal. He wasn't sure whether he should be worried, or not.

Later that morning he was due another meeting in the capital. The complex wasn't situated far from Naypyidaw. It had been established on the eastern side of the country, close to the Shan Hills. The parallel mountain ranges appeared ridged at dawn and dusk. During the height of the day they shimmered, were ephemeral: appeared transient.

The meeting was to establish his success with the periscope. He had a handful of notes of recent predictions: the worldwide domination of the Chinese, the plethora of fuel-less buses, the collapse of the Parisian Eiffel Tower, three synchronistic views of children playing football in a dusty playground, their shirts worn and torn. He would also tell them of the new animals, the lights in the sky, a newspaper report on the final production of rubber with a date he had been unable to read.

Their enthusiasm drifted between each report. Sometimes they were eager to hear of local issues, other times global. At the last meeting they had been obsessed at what he considered to have been a UFO over the American White House. He had to explain with what seemed like an inordinate amount of difficulty that a UFO did not translate as an extraterrestrial visit.

"A UFO is just that," he said, trying to keep his voice monosyllabic, using as few English words as were necessary. "It's an Unidentified Flying Object. The key word is *Unidentified*. What I saw was unidentifiable by me. This does not mean it is a space ship. It simply means it was unidentified."

He had taken the photograph of the tap out of his pocket with the intention of showing it to them as an example of what can be seen and what cannot be seen; but glancing at it before he handed it around he realised that the silver curvature resembled a UFO itself at one angle, and quickly he pocketed it again. Then cursed himself for calling it a *UFO* when quite clearly he could identify it, as it was himself who had taken the photograph.

In his other pocket his wallet contained a photograph of Hlaing taken whilst she slept. She was unrecognisable. He had taken time to position himself carefully for the shot. The arc of her back, the base of her neck, the rise of a buttock. They had been sleeping together and when he returned from the bathroom the image had seemed so perfect that he had to immortalise it. When he showed it to Hlaing she hadn't been sure it was herself. It was another example of what can and can't be seen. For a while afterwards she became convinced he had photographed another woman, and whilst their relationship hadn't frosted, he wondered if the photograph had captured a part of her that had subsequently been lost.

In his house he also had another photo of Hlaing. One that was grainy black and white, a fuzzy close up. Her head was in profile, her short black hair cutting a distinct edge against the lower part of her face. One eye was pressed to the fisheye at his front door. His security camera had captured the image when he was out and he had only seen it on his return from work.

Like the security camera, a periscope is an instrument for observation from a concealed position. Unlike the security camera, the common periscope is a simple construction: a tube with mirrors at both ends set parallel to each other at a forty-five degree angle. Dr Swe Swe Win's periscope was also of such a simple design. What wasn't simple—what was totally unexplainable—were the images that he received when he looked into it.

A house fire—possibly central European. A train crash—most certainly Japanese. A city filled with skyscrapers and low flying aircraft. A shop selling human flesh. A children's activity area, a military zone, a wasteland. A barrel with an indistinguishable word written on one side in large yellow letters. A discothèque impossible to pinpoint without sound. The interior of someone's mouth—possibly at the dentist, maybe in torture. Once: the decapitation of their current political leader. Some images he didn't write down. Others he replaced.

From the sublime to the mundane: each and every image came from the future. He somehow knew this: that nothing came from the past. Yet it was impossible to say for certain other than he had convinced himself of the fact as a necessity to maintain his funding. No one was interested in events that had already happened. Everyone wanted to know what was to come.

Yet. Dr Swe Swe Win paused in his musings as he rode the bus to the capital. He sighed. Squeezed his eyes tight. Ran a hand through that thick black hair of his. Like the Western tale of the *Emperor's New Clothes*, no one dared counteract the visions, few raised questions over their authenticity. The fact that each image came without date didn't concern them. Whilst they did want to know the future, they were also afraid of it. With many of the images, they were glad that they didn't know when or where they might occur.

His house, his wealth and social status: it all floated on a bamboo raft on Inle River. The slightest upset and underwater he would go.

A submarine's periscope was more complex than a simple periscope. Prisms were used instead of mirrors, provided magnification, like two telescopes pointed into each other. If they both had different individual magnification then the difference between them caused an overall magnification or reduction.

But even looking through a submarine's periscope couldn't pinpoint the exact nature of the future. Dr Swe Swe Win had tried on numerous occasions to perfect the process, until he had realised that it was unnecessary. Sometimes it was even unnecessary to look through the periscope. He could write his answers on pieces of paper and pop them into the air tubes from his own imagination.

Even if, occasionally, that felt like cheating.

"You cheated," Hlaing had said.

"No, you cheated," he had said.

It was true. They had both cheated. The periscope told him so.

Sometimes when he dreamt and awoke he couldn't be sure that he hadn't dreamt through the periscope.

Sometimes he wondered whether the periscope was a state of mind, and not a physical object at all—that the physical object was the rationale behind his condition.

Maybe he was no more than a fortune teller, a shaman. Strange how the word *shaman* had come to mean something that was false, rather than something that might be true. The future was held on a delicate balance of semantics.

His meeting in the city had been brief. The officials had nodded, one of them had yawned. They had asked their usual questions—tripped around mentioning their own names—and then confirmed he could leave and his work could continue. Despite the air-conditioning within the building, his shirt stuck to his back before he re-entered the humidity of the outside air.

Hlaing telephoned him as he rode home. Passenger proximity affected his answers.

"I missed your message," she said. "Did you want me?"

"I did," he said.

"What did you want?"

"You."

"I can hear traffic noises. You're still on the bus?"

"Yes."

"Do you love me?"

"Yes."

A giggle. "Tell me you love me."

"I can't."

A laugh. "You're too shy. Tell me you love me when you get home."

"I will."

"Bye."

"Bye."

He turned off his phone for the remainder of the journey.

It was only through his dreams that he saw futures with himself and Hlaing. Always twisting, always conflicting.

Greenery hit the sides of the bus. Vegetation attack. The humidity hung in the air—an almost palpable concoction of moist odours. He imagined both the humidity and the passengers were the ingredients in the *mohinga*. Maybe he would play the role of the onion—a vegetable long associated with fortune telling properties. By circuitous routes, through unfathomable possibilities, each and every one of the passengers together with all the moisture in the air, had arrived at this point simultaneously just for him to have that thought. The staggeringly infinite possibilities of even this one instance terrified him. The future, in comparison, was suddenly impossible to imagine. And—by that very thought alone—*became* impossible to imagine.

Just as it was impossible to imagine that he had loved Hlaing or that he could ever love Hlaing. Just as it was impossible to imagine that he could ever tell Hlaing that he didn't love her.

They came for him several days later. Whatever it was that he had been doing and which he could no longer do, Dr Swe Swe Win realised that somehow they *had* been able to predict the future from his visions through the periscope.

Simply because they were no longer able to do so, once he was no longer able to do so.

But they didn't come with violence, they didn't come angry. They came to plead that he continue with his work. That the loss of his vision might only be temporary. That he should not reveal this loss to the outside world.

He had nodded and thought of his house and the trappings of wealth and told them he was sure the blip was just that. Temporary.

Yet this in itself was a vision seen through the periscope. As was Hlaing. As were the Chinese Americans talking American English. As was the rhinoceros that nearly ran him off the ill-lit road. As was the airtube which carried his scribblings to unseen parts of the complex, as were his journeys to Naypyidaw, as were the visions of human flesh being sold from street stalls, as were the children kicking footballs in the dust. From the UFO to the IFO those futures were either fabricated or predicted the first and only time he looked through the periscope.

Which he then put down, before deliberating what he should do.

Or could do.

Or would do.

Because there were also infinite possibilities which contained none of this.

Monster Girl

That morning, there was an Escher of birds in the sky.

Looking askance it was hard to tell where one ended and another began. They dipped and soared, like a thin piece of fabric caught on the breeze: one object interlinked by individual cells. Yoshi noticed them as he left the train at Yūrakuchō Station. The commuters around him stared ahead, focussed on their destinations, their work. But Yoshi saw the birds, and whilst they were of one colour the black and white tessellates of Escher's print came to mind. Opposites reflected. The same. But not the same.

With a flick of his imagination they were gone.

His satchel slung over his shoulder, he wandered over to the Yūrakuchō Center Building. When he started university his parents had ensured his financial security. He didn't need the host club job, they would have reasoned. And *he* reasoned that he didn't need to tell them. But the job paid for the Krusty Kreme donuts that he bought from the outlet within the center. They were his only extravagance, his remaining earnings were stored in his second savings account: the fund that would engage him a love doll.

He pushed through the floor-to-ceiling glass doors of the bakery, selected a winter-iced heart-shaped donut, and watched the impassive face of the girl behind the counter as it was boxed.

When she passed him the container she smiled. An illusion broken.

Yoshi returned to the train station, headed for the University of Tokyo. He ate the donut in the grounds: the sickly, over-sugared taste oozing into his stomach, lining it for the remainder of the day. *Plastic Beach* played in his earphones. The other students walked on by, in pairs or groups. If they saw Yoshi, it didn't register. He was an outsider here, kept himself to himself. He didn't like attention for attention's sake.

Yoshi was the only student at the host club. The others had dedicated this slice of their lives to their work, as though they might do it in perpetuity. In practice, of course, hosts were usually 'retired' by their late twenties. His persona altered as soon as he slipped into the manned door at the back. In the dressing room he gelled his hair, chatted amiably with the other hosts. A side bet ran around the room as to who would be chosen first. Yet Yoshi knew who would choose him and when. Ayako would arrive later than some, perhaps after one, maybe two in the morning. A *keep bottle* was already reserved for him. He liked Ayako, but the nature of the job meant their relationship was preserved solely within dark corners and neon lights. No drama. It was exactly the way Yoshi wanted it. He liked her enough to tolerate her, little more.

Mid-way through the evening, smart suited and smiling, he joined Shoichi's table. As usual, it was noisy. Yoshi didn't recognise the girl Shoichi was with but she was so drunk she had fallen over. Shoichi reached under her arms, pulled her back onto the leather seat. He pressed the champagne bottle into her hand and she necked it back, white frothing each corner of her mouth like an incoming tide. Yet like the Escher birds, the champagne flowed in one direction whilst giving the impression of the other.

It was then that Ayako tapped him on the shoulder.

He would encourage her to buy drinks whilst she talked about her work, her colleagues, what dresses she had seen and intended to buy, what her husband did for her and what he didn't do for her. This latter part of the conversation edging out slowly—like a spy sneaking a peak at a mark around the corner of a building—only towards the end of the evening. Yoshi nodded. Agreed with everything she said. Listened.

That was what he was good at, listening.

Ayako was good at talking. But then she also wasn't good enough at talking for Yoshi, because, truth be told, she talked too much.

Dawn hit the sky, as swift as a magician pulling a tablecloth out from under a table, retaining everything as it was without the dark background. Shoichi thumped Yoshi hard on the back, a friendly gesture. He ran off, clutching his earnings, his winnings. Yoshi slipped his own payment deep into his trouser pocket. It was Saturday morning. After returning to his apartment and finding time to sleep, he woke and took a train to Saitama Prefecture's Nishi Kawaguchi district.

There wasn't the commuter press at the weekend. The train blurred the landscape outside, yet within the occupants were effectively static. Yoshi fixed his eye on a girl who sat at the far end, diagonally from himself. Her face dipped downwards, immersed in a book. From time to time her eyelashes flickered. The remainder of the blink unseen. When she turned pages, her fingers appeared delicate, as though they too were made of paper. Shoulder-length hair completed her facial ensemble. Yet when she stood to exit Yoshi knew that she would disappoint.

As she left he tried to catch the name of the author she had been reading. Too late, her feet hit the platform and she was off. Released into reality.

Yoshi had cultivated a business relationship with a gentleman by the name of Takashi who he had contacted through an advert in the back of *Aidroid* magazine. When the train came to his stop he stood, disembarked in the same manner as the girl had left the train, turned to his right, and walked the mile to Takashi's workshop.

Takashi had promised him the usual standard for less. Yoshi's love doll should cost him no more than 500,000 Yen. Following confirmation of his satisfaction the doll would be shipped discretely to his apartment. His specifications would be adhered to. 100% silicone, height: 155cm, weight: 27kg, bust: 90 cm with a 65 cm underbust, waist: 58 cm, hips: 80cm, shoe size 23cm. Yoshi had been very precise when they first met. Takashi had been impressed.

"You know what you want, young sir."

Yoshi had shrugged.

"Yet," and here Takashi paused, "are you totally sure about the nipples, the vagina?"

Yoshi placed a finger on his own lips. His silence spoke more than words.

Takashi nodded. No doubt the boy had his reasons.

Almost four months later, Yoshi saw his hand reach out, depress Takashi's door bell. His heart pounding. First date.

૭

"You are quiet tonight Yoshi."

He snapped from his reverie, like a fish breaking free from a taut line.

"Sorry, Ayako." His smile returned, shored up with bamboo scaffolding. In truth, he was back at his apartment, superimposing his doll over Ayako's features, making the comparison, confirming the choice.

He had named her Mimette. Right now; exactly now; she was sitting cross-legged on a purple bean bag, wearing white leggings and a thin cream blouse, slightly bunched around the neckline, a taffeta-effect, watching television. He had placed the volume on low. Her eyes would be open, drinking in the adverts, the game shows. Although she wouldn't actually be watching anything. She would simply be waiting. Waiting for Yoshi's return.

Here, at the host club, Ayako was animated. She had drunk too much. A champagne tower, using six bottles, had recently collapsed. Yoshi had watched in slow motion as the alcohol poured and puddled on the floor. The cost of two Mimette's. It was nothing to Ayako. But he wasn't attracted to her because of the money. He wasn't attracted to her.

Her eyebrows were off-kilter, one marginally higher than the other. Her mouth, usually soft and tender, could sometimes draw a hard line when the dawn flecked the horizon and she realised she had stayed longer than intended. Whilst Ayako was only ever angry with herself, Mimette was angry with no one.

This is what Yoshi was thinking as Ayako chided him for drifting away from her.

At the bar, the owner caught Yoshi's eye. It was enough. Yoshi smiled. Made a remark. Ayako laughed. Stability restored. But it was tenuous, that stability, so easily cracked in reality.

It had been a Wednesday night. Yoshi had barely slept four hours before he was riding the Yamamonte line, heading towards the university. Mimette had lain beside him as he slept. Not touching. Her back facing his back, her face to the wall. Clothed.

Yoshi's parents had quizzed him about his studies, as they did at least once a month. Truth was, he was slipping. Now he had Mimette the opening possibilities of a degree and entrance to business didn't entice. He told his parents enough to make them proud of him. He still withheld information about the host club. Maybe he wouldn't remain there. It ate too much of his time and he no longer needed the money.

On a bench he ate a Krusty Kreme donut purchased the day before. His fridge temperature had hardened the icing, stiffened the dough. He broke it into two pieces. Crumbs drew the attention of pigeons. One speckled black, the other speckled white. Or maybe the opposite. Yoshi looked at the crumbs in his hand. Threw them out.

There was a depression on the surface of the bench. When he turned, he saw Minori for the first time.

Before he knew it, he held out the second half of the Krusty Kreme donut.

Before she knew it, she took it. Icing creamed her fingers, glazed them. Yoshi looked at those fingers. They were as smooth as silicone.

Yet Minori didn't eat the donut. She pulled it to pieces and the two pigeons were joined by others. In moments, all that was left were sticky beaks. Minori licked her fingers, removed a tissue from her bag, then held out her hand.

"Minori."

Yoshi looked at her fingers. Touched her hand briefly.

"Yoshi."

◌

Friday night he telephoned the host club. For an hour beforehand he ate salted peanuts. His voice was dry, hoarse. The management understood. *Would he be available for work tomorrow?* He might. He could feel the nod at the end of the line. He wasn't sure whether he would go tomorrow. He wasn't sure if he would call again.

Beside him on the kitchen table was a steaming bowl of miso soup. He swallowed slowly, regained his voice.

The television was on in the living quarters. Yoshi wiped the corners of his mouth with a handkerchief, then popped a mint. When he entered the living area, Mimette had her back to him, her eyes open to an advert for new technology. He sat beside her, although she didn't notice.

This close, he could smell her perfume. Her skin waited for his imprint. She was dressed in a smart blouse, long skirt. Dressed a little older than her years. Yoshi reached out, cupped her right breast. It was a smooth ball. No nipple. Beneath the skirt, under the white panties, she was equally smooth. Other than her delicate ears and slightly parted mouth she was holeless. A love doll, not a sex doll. Sometimes Yoshi slept with an arm around her. She moulded against his moving form.

There was a dichotomy between Mimette and Ayako and Minori. Mimette asked for nothing from him, gave everything. Ayako gave everything, asked for nothing. Minori gave nothing, asked for nothing. They had shared more donuts, and eaten none. The birds were finding it harder to fly.

Yoshi turned off the television, hooked his arm under Mimette and took her to bed.

At 4am someone knocked hard on his door.

Yoshi sat up, rubbed his eyes. Mimette was facing the wall. The sheet had slipped from her body, and her smooth rear reflected the moonlight. Again, the knocking; insistent. Yoshi rose, pulled on his boxers, dressing gown. Made his way to the door.

The fisheye revealed Shoichi. Of course, he was drunk. There was a girl under his arm. When Yoshi looked closer, rubbed the fisheye and looked again, he saw it was Ayako. Her eyes were half-closed. She was slumped against Shoichi. He wondered if she were awake.

Shoichi thumped the door so hard that the wood vibrated the tip of Yoshi's nose. Seeing a light come on under his neighbour's door, he slipped the lock, stood back as both of them fell in.

Shoichi lay Ayako on the floor. She might be dead. Dead drunk.

"She came for you," he said, as though it explained everything. Then he saw Yoshi's glance to the half-opened bedroom door. "Ah," he said. "We should leave."

Yoshi almost said, *it isn't what you think*. Then decided the alternative was the worse of two evils. Instead he said, "She can't stay here."

"Tell that to her," Shoichi said. "She was crying. Haven't you seen your messages?"

Yoshi glanced over to his house phone, where a green light flashed on and off, a demented stop/go sign. The club had been persistent.

Too far, he heard Shoichi say. *Too far*.

Then Shoichi was pouring himself a glass of water in the kitchen. The sound was so clear, the cup so low beneath the tap, that Yoshi first thought he was peeing.

"You shouldn't have brought her here," he said. "What about her husband?"

Shoichi laughed. "You are her husband," he said. "We are all husbands in the host bar. All perfect. All listen. What does she want with a husband when she has you?"

Yoshi placed his head in his hands. Shoichi slapped his back.

"I'll give her this water. Get her out. Your secret is safe with me."

But it wasn't. Because when they looked to the doorway Ayako was gone, and almost in that same instant there was a keening, a wail of sorrow, and then a moment where self-pity turned to anger, and Ayako's voice could be heard shouting *monster, monster*. Over and over again.

Yoshi suspected it was more a fear of rejection than of what she had seen which had caused Ayako's reaction. Fear of the known, rather than the unknown. This was what women were afraid of nowadays, had always been afraid of. Shoichi bundled her out of the flat, a grin on his face. It wasn't clear why. Fifty-fifty. Even so, Yoshi knew he wouldn't be welcome at the host club again. He would have to focus on his studies if he wanted to make money.

Mimette wasn't damaged, yet her limbs were twisted unnaturally. Yoshi turned on the bedroom light, returned them to a more positive shape. He dressed her, seated her on a stool in the kitchen, then returned to his bed. Wondered if he would dream of Minori.

He did. She was on the university bench with a hand outstretched towards the pigeons. What he thought were crumbs speckling her palm turned out on closer glance to be tears in the silicone from a dozen pigeon pecks. He ran a thumb over Minori's left eye and it failed to close. He ran a quick glance over her blouse, believed he saw the nub of something pressed against the fabric. Then he awoke.

It was somehow still dark. Yoshi wandered back into the kitchen. His mouth had never recovered from the peanuts. On Mimette's left cheek a black shape discoloured her face. Turning on the light, he saw the slug, no more than a few millimetres, antenna extended, as though an alien being receiving signals from outer space.

By the time Yoshi plucked up courage to invite Minori to his apartment, Mimette had already moved on.

Beyond the Island of the Dolls

Stewart awoke to find his shirt damp with sweat. The night was humid. Each breath took an effort, each effort took a breath. Outside his room, moths and mosquitoes were attracted to a naked bulb hung from a wire, like seeds from a blown dandelion. The bulb's light split horizontally through the slats in the blinds, hit the opposite wall silhouetting a grill. Stewart absorbed this within an instant, then reached out for the doll which he knew lay adjacent on the bed.

His fingers enclosed around the plastic arm, the clenched fist. He held the image in his mind. Under his touch the plastic warmed, but didn't soften. He closed his eyes again, fought the urge to believe it was Monica's hand; then the thickness of the heat enfolded him and almost without realising it he slipped back into sleep.

Morning was announced by activity outside his room. Fires burnt. Smoke coerced its way inside, slipstreaming the light. Low voices chatted at the periphery of Stewart's hearing: susurrations. Cooking smells stirred first his nostrils, then his belly. The air was still humid, although without the push of the dark it felt less oppressive. Stewart sat up, his shirt peeling away from the damp sheet. On the bed, the doll remained motionless. Its eyes returning a familiar, static, gaze.

Stewart splashed water over his face from a tin bowl in the corner of the room. There was no mirror so he shaved as best he could; the blade new and sharp, the lubricating strip leaving a snail's trail viscosity on his skin. Stripping off his shirt and dropping his shorts he ran a wet towel over his body. There was little point in changing clothes: the humidity would quickly regenerate a campfire odour. It was easier to dress as he had been; to remain as he was.

Stewart had arrived at the guesthouse in the Mexican borough of Xochimilco late the previous evening, and been ushered to his room by a dusky man with a rough voice and a brusque manner. He had paid only cursory attention to the buildings, but in daylight saw eight rooms that led off the central hub of the courtyard. It was in the courtyard that a communal breakfast was being prepared for the workers and guests: *huevos rancheros*. Stewart was hungry enough to eat, so he dug in, savouring the eggs, tomatoes, peppers and chillies in his burrito, wondering whether he should smile at his fellow men or maintain some distance. By and large, they paid no attention to him. A young girl filled his cup with water and stepped back, courteously. Even though there was no resemblance to Monica, Stewart couldn't help make a comparison, and—with it—a hopeful connection. But the girl was just a girl, and she continued round the group, no more interested in him than the others.

He closed his eyes tight, squeezed out the vestiges of sleep masquerading as tears. Then he stood, returned to his room, and packed a small day sack. He placed the doll on top, bedded on a cushion he used for long bus journeys, then zipped the holdall like a body bag as the doll looked, unblinking, up at his face.

Five months earlier, Stewart's daughter, Monica, aged three years and a handful of months, wrested her hand from his and ran towards Earlham Park Lake to show him her reflection. The grass had been recently cut and was wet after rain—the smell of it hung in the air and reminded him of other days, other grass, other rain. Stewart didn't run after her. Instead he closed his eyes for a moment, savouring the smell and the memories. Then he bent and picked up the doll she had dropped.

In that moment—or fractions either side of it—Monica had slid on the grass, her feet shooting out beneath her like an Olympic luger. Her head fell backwards onto the ground, hit a rock that had evolved a million years for that purpose, and her small body continued concussed, horizontally, flicking up grass cuttings in mimicry of a ticker tape parade, before she reached the lake and slid beneath the water.

Stewart had only heard a faint noise, like the crack of a knuckle joint, then a soft baby sound—almost a wisp of breath—before the smooth splash as Monica entered the lake.

He looked up, the doll's fist in his, and ran.

Yet even before the first step he understood he was late; and that the event had been fated to conclude this way. Not just because he'd closed his eyes, or picked up the doll, but through the accumulation of every decision since his birth which had led to this moment: wading into the murky lake, his hands spooning the water, a desperate search for the daughter that he loved.

And in that futile search he became aware that all subsequent actions would be coloured by the events that happened that day. That his life, in fact, peaked the moment Monica entered the lake. The past was instantly pre-death, the future post-death. Post-marriage to boot, because Amanda would never forgive him.

These thoughts swept into his mind in an instant: complete, intact. It was as though this was always likely to happen, and his responses had been readied in a locked compartment in his mind, waiting for her death to act as the key.

Regardless of the months now past, Stewart found himself in Mexico; alone. He stood—alive—under a hot sun, his belly full of breakfast, his wallet full of pesos. He'd had new experiences. None of which were shared with Monica or Amanda. He didn't know what to think of this.

There was an expression he was aware of, and he felt that it applied. *He was a ghost of his former self.*

Travelling freed him. Once Amanda understood what Stewart already knew, that she could do nothing but blame him for the tragedy, Stewart resigned from his job at the bank and determined to live his life in reverse, accomplishing all he should have done before Amanda and Monica had tethered his reality. Yet, he did this listlessly, marking down days until his own death, at which point he hoped to find some release.

It was outside Laredo, on the US-Mexican border, where another traveller, Guy Malden, had glimpsed Stewart's doll and without knowing of Monica's death had related the story of *La Isla de la Muñecas*.

Stewart dragged on a borrowed cigarette. Malden flicked ash onto the dusty street. They sat on the sidewalk, beers beside them. They had already exchanged coincidences over their film star names. Malden glad he wasn't a Karl, Stewart pleased he was a James. They exchanged anecdotes of travel—although Stewart's felt second-hand, recounted rather than from direct experience. Then Stewart had fished in his bag for something he could no longer remember and Malden had seen the doll.

"That reminds me. There's this island, Jimmy, called *La Isla de la Muñecas*. The Island of the Dolls. It's located on Teshuilo Lake, between Xochimilco and Mexico City. Story goes three girls were playing when one of them drowned. Of course, the locals claim it to be haunted and then this loner, I don't remember his name, sets up camp there and builds a shrine to the girl out of old and broken dolls. Weird, creepy place. These dolls are strung up from tree to tree: eyes missing, limbs missing. Just like a horror movie, you know? Then the guy dies and there's rumours—nonsense stuff—like the dolls came alive and killed him or he went crazy and drowned. Suddenly it's a tourist attraction. I guess there's no accounting for taste."

Malden sparked up another cigarette, the tip glowed red.

Within Stewart, there was a second spark. He crossed the border the following day.

Now he stood negotiating the cost of a trajineras at the edge of Teshuilo Lake. Despite Malden being correct in that it was a tourist attraction, the number of tourists was still small enough to make it a private excursion. And some of the boatmen did not want to go there. Finally, Stewart paid over the odds and climbed onto the brightly painted trajineras. A trestle table ran the length of the boat, with wooden chairs either side. Despite the incongruity of the situation, Stewart was reminded of sitting outside an English pub. He imagined the name of the boat, painted in bright colours in an arch, as *Amanda*, rather than *Lupita*, as it was.

Amanda sat on the other side of the table and raised a glass of lager. "Cheers!"

Monica lay on her back in her pram, fast asleep, hands either side of her head. Perfect.

Stewart held the never-named doll tightly as the boat traversed the tranquil surface of the lake.

The boatman couldn't help notice the doll, but he said nothing.

Stewart felt self-conscious. He wasn't sure if he were approaching the island in an act of appeasement or curiosity. He could argue he was drawn to the island due to the obvious parallels of Monica's death, yet he pushed this argument out of his head. Contextualising it this way seemed to trivialise what had happened. Just as in everything, the death overshadowed him. He couldn't be himself without it, yet wasn't himself after it.

The small wooden jetty welcomed the boat. If this were a horror movie, Stewart mused, the jetty would be shrouded in mist. But the day was bright and clear—a carnival day. It couldn't be brighter if it tried.

Stewart clutched the doll close as he moved from boat to jetty—the watery gap making him fearful. After seeking assurances from the boatman that he would wait, Stewart made a tour of the island.

Malden had been right, it *was* creepy. Dolls festooned the trees attached by thin wire. The climate hadn't been kind to them. Gazing with blank eyes their mostly naked bodies were filthy, dismembered. Headless dolls hung beside limbless dolls beside Barbie's with wild hair and manic expressions. Many gaped, their faces half crushed, plastic burnt. Tiny holes perforated bald heads where hair had once been threaded, what clothes did exist were ragged, torn, incomplete. Yet Stewart didn't shiver. He toured the island fascinated, found himself in a pre-Monica state of interest. Any plans he had of placing Monica's doll amongst the brethren which haunted the island had dissipated. She didn't belong here, she was too clean, too well-kempt. These dolls had been hooked out of the lake, bore the plastic equivalent of a decomposed state. Or they had been donated by the poor populace in exchange for produce from the now neglected vegetable garden. Monica's doll belonged here no more than did Monica herself. No more than did Stewart.

He walked back to the trajineras expecting the boatman to be taking a siesta, but he was awake and waiting. In silence they journeyed across the placid lake to the mainland.

"We can make it horrific if we want to," Esteban Velázquez said. "Everything is light and dark. But if we choose to look at the light, then the darkness is dispelled."

It was two days after Stewart's trip to the island, and he found himself talking to the *mayordomo* of Xochimilco at the newly built shrine to the *Niñopa*.

"Those dolls on *La Isla de la Muñecas*," continued Esteban, "they appear horrific because of their physical state, because they remind us of children, because our minds find it hard to differentiate between the child and the doll. Yet they have simply been neglected. Those exact same dolls, when new, would have been on similar displays within the four walls of a department store. It is only out of context that they appear horrific. And our imagination does the rest."

Stewart nodded. Upon his return from the island he had stayed a second night at the guesthouse and then from casual conversation with the owner—who no longer appeared quite so abrasive—he had been directed to the house of the *mayordomo*.

"We have another tradition," Esteban informed him, "that of the *rosca de reyes*. This originated in France, before the revolution. A lima bean was placed in bread, whoever found it would receive a gift. When the tradition moved to the Americas it was altered and changed according to our customs, until it eventually became the *rosca* we celebrate today. Here the *rosca* is decorated with pieces of orange and lime, and is filled with nuts, figs, and cherries. They serve it with hot chocolate.

"So every year, on January 6th, families all across Mexico gather around their tables to share the *rosca de reyes*. And now, instead of finding a lima bean in the bread, a little plastic doll representing Jesus is hidden there. The person who receives this doll has to make the tamales used in the *fiesta de la Candelaria* on February 2nd. This celebration is the last of the Christmas festivities, forty days after Jesus's birth. So you see, the presence of the tiny doll is a celebration. You should consider that when you look at your own doll, the doll of your child who died."

Stewart wondered what Monica might make of such a festival. There were comparisons with placing a silver sixpence in a Christmas pudding. His own mother had taken to using fifty pence pieces, then latterly pound coins wrapped in tin-foil for hygiene. Monica had been too young to know of it; Amanda had been too dismissive.

He gestured to the image of the child Jesus, known as the *Niñopa*, cradled in the centre of the shrine. "It's this doll I've come to talk about."

Esteban smiled benevolently. "Are you religious, Mr Stewart?"

Stewart carefully considered his answer. "I find it hard to be religious," he said, "following the death of my daughter."

"This image," said the *mayordomo*, "is over 435 years old. Older than your grandfather and his grandfather and his grandfather. Does this not tell us something about immortality? Each February 2nd this 16th century icon—which closely resembles a doll, does it not?—is handed from one *mayordomo* to another. As you can see, this year it is my turn. I have waited decades for the privilege. I am a volunteer, like the others. I paid from my own pocket to build this shrine. I sponsor all the events dedicated to this image. During the year, the image visits homes and hospitals, accompanied by Chinelos dancers. In the death of Jesus, we celebrate life. This is what fuels religion: life now, and life after death."

Esteban reached over and took Stewart's doll from his grasp before he could object.

"This doll is a symbol to you of all you have lost, yet consider it differently. Consider it a symbol of all that you had. You came to Xochimilco to hang this doll from a tree, perhaps as a warning or a threat, as a symbol of death. But instead you should care for it, tend it, as a symbol of life. Just as we do, here in Xochimilco. Even Julián Santana Barrera, who tended the dolls on the island, did so to keep away evil spirits and to appease the girl who had drowned. The dolls there do not represent death unless we wish to see them that way. Man often sees death where it is not."

He handed the doll back to Stewart. When Stewart took it, he sensed a change.

Yet there was no change. Regardless of *La Isla de la Muñecas*, regardless of the image of the *Niñopa* or the story of the baby jesus inside the bread, the unalterable fact was that Monica had died and any attempt to understand it was simply a placebo for Stewart's aching heart.

That was the horror.

It was a horror that transcended boundaries. The horror of death. Yet to know horror you had to experience it, and to experience death meant to no longer know it. In a sense, death was a victimless horror, for once dead *a victim* no longer *is*. Stewart only served to perpetuate the horror by proxy, hadn't cauterised his memories. Just as with the accident, he had only himself to blame.

Outside Esteban's shrine, the sun fought with the sky. Rays penetrated the Earth; touched everything in depth. Stewart looked up, shielded his eyes, yet even then the glare was so intense that he had to divert his gaze.

And then, from his scorched eyes, the street bleached back into view. Dusty white buildings, motorcycles, battered cars, a *churros* stall. A negative restored after a burn. A small figure stood on the sidewalk, blurred, elongated, thin. As his eyes readjusted, so the figure refocused. It wasn't Monica, of course; it could never be.

Stewart still held the doll in his hands. He understood Esteban's reasoning, that he should consider it an object of remembrance and celebration as an aid to forgetting. Yet it wasn't enough. He had projected Monica onto the doll; they were one and the same. And the doll could feel no more horror than she.

Fiercely he clutched her, close to his chest. The dusty road stretched like blown debris, like ashes, to the horizon.

Rain from a Clear Blue Sky

I arrived at the pub in the company of Sebastian, his straw-blond hair flicked from side to side as he looked left and right for his friends.

Myself, Sebastian, Sergei and Paula had not long returned from a week long hike in the Hindu Kush mountain range; that bordering Pakistan rather than the Afghanistan side. The trip had been beset with dangers—both logistically and from the locals. Our problems only started with the mountains themselves. Despite Paula's carefully chosen clothes and deliberately close-cut haircut she still experienced difficulties with the male population. I found I had to keep close to her side to ensure her safety. For all of us, Paula was more of a challenge than the trek, but everything paid off and so here we were, back in London once again, on a Saturday afternoon at the Cittie of Yorke pub in High Holborn.

Conversation flowed with the beer. It wasn't long before empty glasses reflected each other on the wet surface of the circular table, and we were enthusing over what had been and considering where to go next.

"We need a challenge," Sebastian said, ever the adventurer. "We need something more than just a mountain. We need to push ourselves further."

Paula smiled, knowingly; although even she couldn't imagine what was to come.

Sergei coughed and mumbled something into his half-empty glass, the words echoing round the rim before they fell hidden in the depths of his Sam Smiths. I turned to look at him, but he didn't notice.

"What was that?" Paula asked.

"The Dyatlov Pass," Sergei repeated, lifting his mouth from his glass. "I think we should try the Dyatlov pass."

"Maybe we would if we knew what it was." Sebastian downed the remainder of his beer, stood unsteadily, and meandered over to the back of the pub and the toilet.

Paula leant forwards, almost brushing against me, interested. "The Dyatlov pass? Why do I know that name?"

Sergei opened his mouth, burped unexpectedly, apologised, and then said: "Why wouldn't you? It's infamous."

I knew what he meant, because I was aware of the pass. The route was a ski trek across the Northern Urals, named after the leader of a ski party who came to a mysterious end in the late 50s. The pass was on the eastern side of a mountain called Kholat Syakhl—a local Mansi name meaning *Mountain of the Dead.*

"Infamous?"

Sergei shook his head. "In a moment," he slurred. He returned his glass to the table where it skated a few millimetres before coming to a stop. He ran a calloused hand through his thick black hair. Wiped his nose. Paula sat back, bemused, then glanced across to where I was sitting, her brow furrowing ever so slightly in puzzlement. She was about to speak when Sergei added, "Wait for Sebastian."

It wasn't long before he returned, his hands full of drinks.

"Come on then," he said. "What's with this pass?"

Sergei sipped the new beer, grimaced as though the taste was unfavourable, then promptly drank down a third.

"Subzero temperatures, a two week trip. There's a history, though; something happened there over fifty years ago which dissuades people from attempting it. But I think we should go. Where eagles fear to tread."

Sebastian gave a warm laugh, the beer edging over the rim of his glass and onto his fingers. He leant over to a nearby table and picked up a beer mat—ours had been shredded over the course of the afternoon—before putting his glass down and licking his fingers. "That's *Where Eagles Dare*; the movie. What's the other reference?"

Paula smiled. "Where angels fear to tread."

"Whatever," Sergei said. So then there was no more to say. It was always like this. This was how trips were decided.

As usual, Sebastian took care of the legal documentation, assisted in Russian by Sergei who also arranged the travel arrangements. Paula took care of the equipment, clothing and food. Layers were essential: regulating body temperature was the main concern. And with regards to food, whilst this wouldn't be obvious to a layman, anything with a high water content needed to be avoided. The lower the water content, the less likely it would freeze. Dehydrated soup, instant cereal mixes, granola bars: these would be the staples for the duration of the trek. And in the absence of anything else, they might even be enjoyable.

Sergei had said, and Sebastian had it confirmed, that the temperature might range between minus ten and minus thirty degrees centigrade. Hiking in those conditions could mean burning an additional five hundred calories daily. Layers of clothing prevented using excessive calories to keep warm, but the body would be running at full blast to keep the core temperature within reasonable limits together with the physical effort involved with walking and skiing. Grazing would be necessary: stopping to eat a larger meal would simply drop body temperature and cause a rapid cooling of fingers and toes. In fact, every task involved in preparing food needed to be thought through by Paula in the comfort of her own home whilst imagining what it would be like doing the same tasks wearing mittens like boxing gloves.

I hung around Sebastian more than the others over the following weeks. He tended to get nervous before each trip, deliberated as to whether to pull out—more playing with the idea rather than seriously considering it; as if the yes/no situation excited him. He'd speak to me without expecting any answers: random questions about the validity and sense of the trek, doubts over his ability, over the ability of the others. It didn't matter that it had all been done before. Our group had a ten year history. Each member had grown in that time: in confidence, ability and strength. But this only meant that we had to be pushed harder in order to be satisfied. When Sebastian pushed against *that*, I knew he was testing himself, and I let him be to confirm his own will.

Five months after the discussion at the Cittie of Yorke—five months of unwavering freelance work to fund the trip, five months of cutting back on everything from beer to nights out to heating bills (which Sergei joked was to get us in the mood for the *subzeroness* of it all)—we arrived by train at Ivdel, a city in the centre of the northern province of Sverdlovsk Oblast in late January. The air was biting cold, it stiffened our clothing. I watched as Paula's breath appeared to hang out of her mouth as she spoke, a visible ghost of her words—an ice bridge—until finally it dissipated into the night. Backpacks already dug uncomfortably into shoulder blades, but the group were used to this transition period. Within a few days it would feel like nothing was being carried at all.

The following morning we took a truck to Vizhai, the last inhabited settlement that far north. Sergei conversed in Russian with the driver as we bumped over the infrequently used roads. We never found out what they were saying, despite their occasional laughter. It was a day later, on the 27th January, that the trek began in earnest. If, five months earlier, a snapshot had been taken of the drinks at the Cittie of Yorke it would have been clear that some of them were finished and some had been left. This would have been an apt reflection of the outcome of the trek.

o

From previous experience we knew the first few days would cement us as individuals and seal the nature of the trip.

The going wasn't hard, but it was strenuous. Walking in snow was laborious; something none of us had done for a while and the brief flurry that had constituted the English winter didn't count. For the moment we carried our skis, it would have been too easy to use them. Sebastian invoked that part of his character which made him gregarious, yet also annoying; relating jokes and incidents as though he were the raconteur in the group but which simply reminded the others that despite all their journeys together they didn't really know him. Paula was the show-off, her faux-femininity at odds with her inner nature. Her hair had returned to mid-shoulder length but was wrapped tight under her hat and her features hardened under the glare of the sun reflected by the white surroundings. Limbering up early morning she would cartwheel, leaving hand and footprints in the snow. *To confuse anyone who follows us*, she laughed. Sergei developed an aloofness which an outsider would put down to his Russian heritage, yet which the others knew was a sometimes disturbing state of withdrawal—a distancing from humans towards a greater affiliation with the landscape. I took on attributes of all three, knowing, as usual, that my place there was guaranteed even if not always accepted. Paula in particular would often look my way with a question in her mouth which she never asked. I'd call it female intuition, if I believed that any such thing existed.

They say the Eskimos have over forty words for snow, although I think that myth has long been debunked. What is clear, however, is that snow demands several words in description. If the landscape was stunning it was because of the snow: that clichéd blanket which makes everything the same. If it fell and covered us we would be indistinct shapes. That thought played on my mind as our journey continued—that at some point, we were indistinguishable.

On 31st January we set up a temporary camp at the edge of the highlands. Items were to be left there for collection on the return journey. It would be the following day we would enter the pass itself. We could see it clearly from where we stood, flanked either side by the mountains. It channelled us. I could see the others thinking the same. That our destination and in default our destinies were linked to it, that we had as much choice entering it as water did swirling down a plug hole.

That night, each cocooned in sleeping bags, several layers of clothing fighting the cold, Paula couldn't help but question Sergei about the incident we had avoided talking about. The incident that, in some ways, had been the instigator for the trip.

"Do you really want to know?"

I watched as the others nodded. I was curious too, although I felt I knew the story.

Sergei told it from the beginning. A group of ten hikers had taken this route in the winter of 1959. They were reduced to nine when one of them had to return due to illness. He was the only one to survive. When the others were discovered the circumstances of their deaths was puzzling. Their tent had been cut open, from the inside out. Footprints—including some barefoot or with one shoe—were evident in the snow. Two bodies were found by the remains of a fire, dressed only in their underwear. Three others had major skull and chest fractures although none of them had external wounds. The body of one, a girl, was missing a tongue.

If it were cold within the tent prior to Sergei recounting the story, I could feel the atmosphere chill before he reached the end. Paula in particular had turned her head away from Sergei, was regarding me with a distasteful glare. Sebastian's head rested on his knees, as though he were sleeping; but I could tell he was very much awake.

"It's a puzzle," continued Sergei. "I have my own theories."

"So have I," Paula snapped. "A body missing a tongue isn't unusual. A scavenging animal would seek out the soft tissue of an open mouth, particularly if it smelt of food." She stuck out her own tongue, almost in jest; not quite. She was clearly shaken.

Sergei was the harbourer of unnerving tales. I remembered one he had told a few years previously: that of the third man.

We had been trekking through Tierra del Fuego National Park heading for the snow-capped mountains of Cadena Sampaio, and the going had been particularly harsh. It had been our first cold weather trip and the nature of our food supplies had been underestimated. Sergei couldn't stop postulating on our possible demise, until Sebastian had shouted at him with such force that Paula swore afterwards she had seen the air move between them.

Later, within the confines of the tent, and aware that the next town was only a day away, Sergei had said, "Shackleton was in this neck of the woods." Sometimes his Russian pronunciation of English phrases endeared him to me, and I would seek out his company more than others. "South Georgia," he continued, "you know where those islands are? Well, there were three in his party, and during an arduous two day march Shackleton claimed that sometimes they were four; not three."

We had looked from one to each other. Was one of us the odd one out? The third man syndrome had been explained to me before. That a group under stress might imagine someone else with them as a comfort; this ranged from groups of climbers to sailors or survivors of shipwrecks, or polar explorers. Some saw it as a coping mechanism, others as a guardian angel. Still others, of course, doubted its veracity at all. But of course, any figures were bound to be incorporeal. I watched Sebastian and Paula closely, as they dismissed it as nonsense; yet still they couldn't help but cast glances about them which they hadn't done previously.

Yet now, away from that Argentinean territory, several years forward, engulfed in a tent near the Dyatlov pass, other superstitions shrouding our surroundings as temporary as the darkness of the night, I wondered again if the others saw any truth in it. Or whether, like rain from a clear blue sky, something that seemed miraculous could easily be scientifically disproved.

Morning came and our tent was intact. No tears from the inside out, no semi-nakedness, no missing tongues. Sebastian was the first to wake. I followed him outside. He stretched as best he could in his multiple layers of clothing, and then went behind the nearest tree to relieve himself. I could see the steam rise skywards as the snow melted. When he finished he stopped and looked at me, maybe surprised to see me standing there, maybe wondering if I'd seen him urinate. Then he shook his head and snuck back into the tent.

I waited for the others to rise. When they had breakfasted, packed their belongings and had everything ready, we approached the entry to the pass.

Sergei couldn't help remind us: "This is where it all went wrong for the Dyatlov nine."

"Shut up."

Paula was getting jittery. I'd seen it happen before, on the Hindu Kush, when we'd walked past a group of what could have been Mujahideen with rifles slung over their shoulders; but all they wanted was to bum smokes and didn't pay her a second glance.

"Seriously," Sebastian said, "what do you think happened?"

His question reminded me that Sergei had a theory no one wanted to listen to the previous evening; tiredness had overtaken the others and he'd been talked down before they slept.

"I mean," Sebastian continued, "there were no external injuries, right? But something hit them. Avalanche?"

Sergei kept his head down, kept walking. I knew that he'd wanted the conversation the previous night, in the dimness of the tent, where the story might have had a more sustained impact. "This area doesn't see a lot of avalanches," he said.

"But it could be, right?" seized Paula. "Maybe that's what bowled the tent over, made it look like it was ripped open. This would explain why they left the tent leaving some of their clothes inside. Hypothermia can lead to a condition where you get confused; I can't remember what that's called. Those who were found in their underwear could have taken off their own clothes. It happens."

Sergei's skis made a swishing sound. The others had stopped.

"Listen Sergei," Sebastian said, "why get precious about it. Come on, tell us your theory."

"Later."

The sky clouded over and snow fell as we entered the pass. The world became monochrome, our shadows became ourselves. Fat flakes covered our goggles and we brushed them off with thick sleeves. In one particular gusty flurry we all became separated for a moment, glimpsing each other as if through the white noise on an analogue TV. Paula saw me first, and kept close; the others were either behind or ahead. When the snow cleared Paula looked around in surprise, Sebastian and Sergei were some way off to her right. I could see confusion behind her goggles, before she headed off towards them.

Sebastian reached into his pack and pulled out granola bars, handed them around. I could tell that Sergei was burning to tell his story—the heat almost insulated him against the biting cold. But he held back. Sebastian was equally eager to ask, yet Paula seemed indifferent, as though her experience in the sudden dense snow had caused her to dwell on other things. As though the snow lay piled in a corner of her mind.

We set off again. The pass could be traversed in a day. As we skied I looked from side to side at the tree-filled landscape. Somewhere along this route the nine members of the Dyatlov incident, Zinaida Kolmogorova, Ludmila Dubinina, Alexander Kolevatov, Rustem Slobodin, Yuri Krivonischenko, Yuri Doroshenko, Nicolai Thibeaux-Brignolles, Alexander Zolotariov and Igor Dyatlov himself, had perished. It was impossible not to imagine their bodies lying under the snow, as if they had never been recovered. But it was important to be respectful and I focussed on my three companions who needed my help more than the dead.

Mid-morning the sky brightened. The weather was so changeable it could catch you unawares. We stopped briefly, and Sebastian set up the camping stove to make soup. He added water from his canister before adding compacted snow, to prevent the bottom of the pan burning through, and when it had melted the dehydrated soup granules went in. The flame wasn't hot enough to warm anyone, yet we grouped around it anyway, like Neanderthals outside of a cave.

"My theory," Sergei began, without warning, "is that one member of the group suffered from Capgras delusion. You know what this is?"

Sebastian shook his head. I knew. Paula did too.

"Isn't that where someone believes a relative or a friend has been replaced by an identical-looking imposter? Freaky. But how does that tie in with what happened?"

Sergei lent on his skis. "Imagine," he said, "if there was some kind of mass delusion. Imagine if this occurred with the Dyatlov party."

Paula shrugged. "But that explains nothing. I can see where you're going with it. That maybe one of them went crazy, thought the others weren't who he believed they should be. But you said yourself there were no outward signs of injury. None of them showed signs of being attacked."

Sergei's eyes narrowed. "What if," he said, "the person who each of them believed had been replaced was themselves. You know what the inquest determined as the cause of death: *a compelling unknown force*. What could be more compelling than suicide?"

Sebastian's *huh* pre-empted Paula's. "You're just complicating things. You throw this stuff into the mix just to unnerve us. God knows why."

"Maybe because it's fun," Sergei said; he bent down to the pot and served out the soup.

"What if it's the third man who develops the Capgras delusion?" I said; but they were no longer interested now the soup was ready to eat. I watched them carefully as they spooned it into their mouths. It hit me then that no matter how long I might stay with them I would never really know them as well as they knew each other.

After they had eaten they packed away the stove and checked their equipment, skis, and goggles, before heading off to complete the second half of the pass.

But I stayed behind. I didn't go with them.

I watched the falling snow obliterate my friends.

Sebastian was the practical one. He had arranged the visas and the associated paperwork. Paula, bless her, had taken on the female role even though she would never have admitted it: kitting out the team and researching the food. Sergei took care of the travel arrangements, but only up to the point of our arrival in Ivdel. When it came to day to day navigation, here on the ground, it was I who held that responsibility. It was up to me to keep them safe.

None of them would have acknowledged this. Because none of them acknowledged me.

For Sergei, the conditions themselves weren't enough. He required something else in the mix, the same way water reinvigorated dehydrated granules. If it wasn't the third man story, then it was the Sasquatch in the Pacific Northwest, or spooking us with a trip to Seneca Creek State Park without telling us what had been filmed there. I knew he'd been determined to get us to this spot just to raise the genuine unsolved Dyatlov incident, then, when we didn't quite bite, he embellished it with the Capgras delusion. But this wasn't the Sergei I had originally met, when he was one of a party of six who had become lost at the edge of Cholomunga's skirt, when he was naïve and inexperienced and needed someone to guide his group back down the mountain. If I thought back to those times I realised I didn't recognise him anymore.

Then again neither was Paula the girl I once knew. Her charm had hardened, she had shed her femininity and forced herself to act like a man in situations where she had come to believe she couldn't survive as a woman. But she was wrong: she needed to be herself and no one else. Cart-wheeling in the snow was *her* yet it wasn't enough, it wasn't consistent. And as for Sebastian, well, Sebastian remained Sebastian. It was on Sebastian, therefore, that I decided to focus my attention.

I headed off into the snow that had begun to fall heavy, just as the wind whipped up and blew it horizontal down the length of the pass. Visibility was poor but it mattered nothing to me. The others, though, might not see the ravine.

What if the third man developed the Capgras delusion? I reminded myself as I journeyed towards them. *What if the third man were not a guardian angel, but malicious? What if there* was *a third man out there, hidden by the snow, who wasn't me?* I entertained myself with these thoughts, but like Sergei's musings they were simply a subterfuge for my real intentions. I no longer believed a third man could split himself in three. I had to save just one, and one alone. The others would have to try to survive without me.

Cling

(Cinema) "makes the invisible visible, the unclear clear, the hidden manifest, the disguised overt, the acted non-acted, the untruth truth."
- Dziga Vertov

In retrospect we did everything backwards. It was Joachim's idea. He thought it was revolutionary but he was just kicking against the pricks. In the same way that he never washed his handkerchief, just transferred it from trouser pocket to jeans pocket to trouser pocket. A deliberate idiosyncrasy to hide his inadequacies. Any excuse to be other than normal.

He knew it was wrong. This is what frustrates me. Start with the trailer. Use it as a marketing tool to gain funding. But the trailer can only be a montage of perfect moments that have to come from the film. So the film *has* to exist. You can't quote from a story that has yet to be written.

Three years later I'm sitting with Jasmine in a hotel room listening to *Polly Scattergood* on my mp3 player whilst she writes poetry.

The windows are open and the sky is blue. Yesterday we stood together before the view. From the street we were framed. No one looked up. It isn't some generic brand hotel in an increasingly generic city; no. We're in a semi-rural location in Greece. Whites and blues, so bright they hurt the eye. Flagstones smoothed with age. But we're not really here.

I'm propped up against the hard pillow. Jasmine has her back to me. Her curves match mine, spooned against each other yet not quite touching. I can just see over her body, witness words forming on the page. When she places the full stop at the end of the poem I wonder whether it needs to be there. Whether it prevents the narrative continuing in the reader's head.

Yesterday she turned twenty-four. For one week we'll be the same age. In synchronicity. But it's all just numbers, the distance between us hasn't changed. The punctuation remains the same.

The hotel room interior reminds me of one in Barcelona, four, maybe five years previous. On that occasion I was sharing with Joachim. Twin beds. Green interior. Dark, not light like this room, but four-sided and unfamiliar all the same. It's not the décor which draws the comparison, but watching Joachim put lines on the page. His great love movie. His post-modernist existential film which will turn the world on its head, make him a stack of money, and be the most original, heart-breaking, outré set of images ever committed to celluloid.

Except, of course, that it wasn't.

Just like our beds in that cheap hotel, it never got made.

You have to be original without trying. I understand that now. In the same way that you never find love when you're looking for it.

Jasmine turns, regards me. The angle slopes her away, as though she is leaving. But she is smiling, and the curve of that smile skis towards the bedclothes and I lift myself up and bend over her, pushing my lips against the corner of her mouth until the displacement of my weight unsettles me and I return to a more comfortable position.

"Don't read it yet," she says, mistakenly believing my eyes were wandering over the poem as we kissed. "It needs an edit."

"So do our lives."

"No more faux movie-speak please."

So we remain like that, barely touching. Honest words falling out of her head like tears onto the page, yet nothing actually being said.

◎

Once Joachim realised he wouldn't get funding by lying back and waiting for it to fall out of the sky he became philosophical about the trailer.

"It's true anyway," he said, after a night of red wine and nonsense, "that the trailer has to be better than the film. Audiences take it for granted that they are, or they wouldn't let themselves be persuaded by trailers time and time again, despite the many tales of disappointment they'll subsequently recount."

"And?" I was growing impatient. It was late and I wanted to be home. Or, at least, walk through the quiet streets of Norwich which at this hour gave themselves up to their surroundings, denuded of people.

He dragged on his joint. "Society doesn't dictate that it's the fault of the trailer if the film fails, rather they see it as the film's fault if it doesn't live up to the promise of the trailer."

I didn't say anything this time. I had no idea where he was going.

"Jesus, Barnaby! It's a metaphor isn't it? It's a fucking metaphor for life."

"I dunno why I metaphor," I said, feeling antagonistic.

He stood. Something whizzed by my head unexpectedly. At least it was the joint and not the bottle.

He shouted: "Do you have to bring Jasmine into everything?"

I shrugged. I hadn't been thinking of Jasmine specifically. But then I did.

She had been a student at the School of Art & Design before it was renamed the Norwich University College of the Arts. Same meat, but potatoes not chips. Joachim, who was at least six years older than us, had placed an advert on the student message boards: *All you need to make a movie is a girl with a gun. We want a girl. We have the gun.*

Jasmine was the only one who replied. I held the business mobile that day and her voice was light, ethereal, yet matter of fact.

"I get the Godard reference, but what is the movie about?"

Stumblingly I tried to explain, but Joachim had held so much back it wasn't even clear to myself what his intentions were.

"So it's malleable, yes?"

Something in the word choice held back my answer. Two auteurs weren't better than one.

"If you mean we can make it up as we go along," I eventually said, "then that's a possibility." I paused, for dramatic effect. "Just like life, of course."

I was young then. And it was the closest I came to a chat up line.

So, Jasmine became part of the film. She was what would be described as unconventionally pretty. Her telephone voice had intimated a slight form, thin arms, elfin hair. Maybe wearing dungarees which were back in fashion, over a Warhol t-shirt. Yet whilst she wasn't the opposite she was different. Two doughnuts too many. Her armpits unshaved. She wore short skirts with black leggings and flowery Doc Martens. If I hadn't already fallen in love with her over the phone, then I fell in love with her when she first walked on set.

To that I beat Joachim, who only fell in love with her through the camera lens.

"We could go out," I said.

"We *are* going out."

She had rolled over on the hotel bed. Her t-shirt had ridden up, exposing her midriff. "We've been going out for the past four years."

Fireworks go out, I thought. *Once they've been fired into the sky.*

"C'mon," I repeated. "Let's go out."

"I'm gonna shower first."

She rolled off the bed. Pulled her t-shirt over her head and slipped out of her shorts. "Coming?"

"In there?" I laughed, for the first time in what seemed like days. The shower wasn't big enough for both of us, even when alone the glass doors were pressed against you like cling film.

"I'll be five minutes."

As the glass steamed, I read her poem.

Later we held hands as we walked, towards the ocean sprawling ahead undulating in the sunlight as though topped with silverfish. The white sails of boats flagged pockets of civilisation. I imagined being on those boats, cutting through the waves, the spray wetting my face, my hair. The movement making me feel alive. Making me feel as though my life was going somewhere.

I wasn't even sure how we connected anymore.

The first time I saw Joachim touch her hand I wanted to punch him. And all he did was step forward, place a cigarette between her fingers, then step backwards. Shielded by the camera.

"She doesn't even smoke," I said.

"She can fight her own battles." He fiddled with the camera. "It's not even lit."

"I am here you know." Jasmine posed.

There were more than the three of us. We were flanked by technicians and lighting men and sound men. I say men, but they were recruited from college. We were just playing roles. Playing at grown ups. Playing at knowing what we were doing. But then we'd all watched movies, we'd all swooned over our personal Scorsese's, or Truffaut's, or Hitchcock's or Polanski's and each and every one of us knew how to film a movie inside our own heads.

But it was Joachim's vision we were following. If only he had one.

The set designer was an art student that I was seeing until I'd realised Jasmine was all I wanted to see. Becky was retro. Watching her collect 70s objects from thrift stalls and house clearances I realised it wouldn't be long before my own object d'art and outmoded appliances would be accumulated by kids believing they were kitsch. In the future I might time travel within an art gallery, seeing the world from the comfort of my living room, once removed.

But Joachim wasted those sets. He didn't realise the quality of the material he was working with. Or maybe he did, yet because it was superior he snubbed it. Like the kid in the park, the film was his ball. We could kick it about, but it remained his ball.

So yes, it came down to metaphor. We all play roles, don't we? We all look back, review the salient points, underscore our lives with the music which meant the most to us. We want to be fiction, maybe because we *are* fiction. Reality is nothing more than a consensus.

I'd met Joachim because he was temporarily part of the writers group which met Wednesday evenings at the *Hog In Armour*. I wanted to be *something*. I needed to *be*. I'd tried poetry, short stories, couldn't make it with the novel. I thought I might be able to paint, to act, to sculpt, to play an instrument. But Joachim noticed my talent straightaway. I could edit.

"Your role," he said, pressing his manuscript into my hands, "is to take this and return it as though nothing has changed. Yet it will be better for it. You're the surgeon with the scalpel, dissecting me as I'm unconscious on the operating table. When I awake, my insides will have changed though the exterior will forever be me. Do you understand?"

"You want me to read through this?" I said. "And make changes?"

"Listen," he gesticulated with his cigarette—it always seemed like he had six fingers on his right hand—"the changes will make themselves, you'll simply be the conduit through which they happen. I've seen you give feedback in the group and you're what I need." He slapped me on the shoulder, as though pinning me to the earth. "I don't give up my work easily."

He didn't. That was the only time we ever mentioned our intellectual transaction. I was the prostitute who took the money before the act. The money that was invisibly passed between us, counted, and carefully put away.

I picked up a stone. Smooth and warm to the touch. Then I threw it into the sea.

Jasmine shielded her eyes against the water.

"It's broken, isn't it?"

"Broken?"

"Everything. It's like a piece of cinema film that's got torn in the projector. The same images are playing over and over again, becoming more ragged and torn as they repeat. Until eventually the light burns through and that's all we're left with. The clarity of the light that blinds."

For a moment I thought she was finally talking about our relationship, to the extent that I had allowed myself the hope of being released. But then I saw that she meant life itself. And I nodded. And suggested the image was perfect for a poem.

"Maybe I should return to acting," she said, answering a different question.

But she had never really acted. Not really. At all.

"Just be yourself," Joachim said.

We were standing in the 70s room. Three-sided, part of the art exhibition which Becky had assembled from her dead grandmother's bric-a-brac. A fortuitous demise. Jasmine was lounging on the sofa. An unlit cigarette in her left hand. A gun in her right. The gun was plastic and looked it. There wasn't much we could do about that. She alternated putting the cigarette and then the gun into her mouth. Because I loved her, I was glad the cigarette was unlit as the gun was unloaded.

She turned to the camera. "What exactly do you want me to do?"

"Cut!" Joachim beamed. "That was perfect. We can use that."

We had begun to film the trailer. Shards of reality slipping together amidst the fabric of fantasy. Joachim had become convinced that if we shot the best bits we could pop the rest in later, once we had the funding. I had a feeling that the arts board viewed things differently. They were after authenticity of expression, not fraudulence. Still, I hankered after continuity. I would play CDs in track order, would read collections of short stories as they came rather than dipping in and out. I wanted to live my life as one experience, and subsequently not view my memories in situ but part of the greater package.

Joachim wanted to capture life differently. In his estimation, the perfect trailer showed the film you have yet to see as the one you would remember if you had already seen it.

It was this difference which ripped at an already decaying, transient, friendship.

I woke one morning with the sun in my eyes. A thin sheet covered us. Cool outside, snug inside. My naked body pressed against Jasmine's. The previous night's lovemaking had been as close to perfect as it ever might be. Jasmine had gasped and I had cried. Deep, resonant tears shook my body that I couldn't explain. My arm was outside the covers, holding her through the sheet, wrapping her as I held her close. Then a stifled cough. I whirled around and saw the glare wasn't the sun's, but an arc light in the corner of the room. Standing nearby were five formless figures, darkened as though in shadow but masked by the arc and my inability to see beyond. Maybe that was my problem, I could never see beyond much at all.

"What the fuck?"

Jasmine sat upright. Squinted but didn't scream. Then she muttered *You bastard*, and lifted the pillow before burying her head underneath it.

Beyond the glow of the arc I heard a scrape; there was a flash of fire, and then the circular burn of a cigarette end. "Just be yourselves," Joachim said.

◌

As we headed away from the beach we stopped before a store window. The display was in transition. Mannequins without shame stood half-dressed, some leaning against each other, others alone, hatted, bare-breasted. We stood separate, reflected in the glass, viewed just as we were viewing. In that reflection my hand reached for Jasmine's extended fingers.

"*Signomi.*"

We were separated by two workmen carrying a square of clouded Perspex. I regarded Jasmine through it, blurred. She turned to face me, her eyes were sunken holes, her mouth opened in a laugh and became a milky void, her arms reached out and punctuated the plastic, pushed through it as though she wore cling-film gloves. By the time the workmen passed I was gasping, out of breath, coughing up sputum at the bottom of the hill.

When I looked back at Jasmine the sun was behind her. The light swallowed her form, made her stick-like as my eyes differentiated her edges. I gulped, placed my hands on my knees, took several deep breaths, then returned to her. Stones sliding under my shoes as I walked back up the hill.

"What was that you were doing?" she asked later, back on the bed, the blinds closed against the heat of the day, beads of sweat breaking from our bodies like bubbles under water.

I shrugged. "I got spooked."

"Spooked?"

"Don't ask me to describe it."

She fanned herself with the notepad containing her poetry.

"It's never left you, has it?"

She wasn't looking at me, but at a point on the wall. It moved. I watched as a cream-coloured lizard ran behind the unopened wardrobe.

"And don't say, *what hasn't,*" she continued. "I hate it when you do that."

I thought it easier to say nothing.

Later, as she slept mid-afternoon, I read her poem again. I wanted a way inside her but it was deliberately obscure. She hid herself behind the words, hid her true self from me. Her poems were supposed to reveal but they obfuscated. I wondered if she knew it.

My back was sticky against my t-shirt against the bedsheet. I got up, stripped, and showered. As Jasmine did before me, I left open the bathroom door, watched her disappear on the bed amid the steam as the hot water ran. Squeezy soap oozed through my fingers. I waited, held my breath, then wiped a clear circle against the glass and wasn't sure if I were relived or disappointed that I could see her.

Following the bedroom incident we encountered Joachim at various inappropriate unscheduled intervals. Never quite as audacious as to appear with the entire crew, nevertheless the whirring of the cine camera accompanied our perfect moments, a subliminal backdrop to our courtship like the chirping of cicadas or traffic noise. I tried to remember the script, to pinpoint where his trailer was skipping past conversations and observations. My continuity interrupted, I found myself in situations without knowing how I had arrived. Even now, three years later, standing bolt upright in this Greek shower, I have no recollection of the plane journey, of our breakfast, of returning to the hotel from the beach.

It's more than feeling part of a movie that was never actually made. Something that Jasmine and I continuously agree upon, in those moments when we cling to each other as though tomorrow has yet to be written. It's more that my life has been edited.

Joachim had been right. When I returned the script to him he couldn't see the changes, but it was better for it.

Even so, it was still his script.

Wounder

Cramped on the single bed in my one room apartment Chloe's head rests on my chest and I try to synchronise our breathing.

Outside, the dawn is rising. My amber curtains become translucent with the emergence of the sun. It was a warm night. Not too hot to be huddled together, yet too cold not to be. Chloe's thin hair is tied back into a ponytail held by pink elastic. I kiss her forehead, taste sodium traces like a deer at a salt lick.

She dreamt the deer overnight. A white hart. Her own heart had beat inside her chest and she pulled up her t-shirt, antlers under the skin pushing out mini-triangles, until suddenly it burst through and skittered left and right, flicking up forest debris with hooves of shining silver. She gave chase—her stomach unquestioningly healed—until the deer stopped by a white lake. She had imagined fish in the lake until the deer's hooves refused to fall through the surface. She watched as it bent its neck, extended its tongue. Just at the point of touching the surface, she woke.

I know all this despite her not telling me.

She knows that I know.

The white hart faded into the whiteness of the lake, became background.

Two hours later, with the top of the sun level with my windowsill, I regulate my breathing until it matches hers. Only it doesn't: she is always one breath ahead or one breath behind.

When I first met Chloe everything was *bonus* or *wounder*. Our favourite band coming to play at The Waterfront. Bonus! The same gig cancelled: wounder! It became habit. Something she—and then we—said repeatedly, a validation of the relationship. The sharing of certain words like a mantra, a secret handshake. Something that was wholly me and wholly her. Something that was *us*. That I would always associate with us.

She was a natural brunette. During summer months her hair colour lightened as her skin colour darkened. We met during Spring, and shortly afterwards her previously one-tone face became speckled with freckles. In my madder moments I imagined that each new freckle was an indication of her increased love for me. I wanted love to manifest itself in ways other than the purely emotional. I see now that she wanted this too, but that the freckles were not part of it.

Due to the death of her previous tutor, our evening digital photography classes had been combined. I saw her first through the lens of my camera, as I was working through the menus, trying to find a setting for multiple exposures which I was sure I had found before yet somehow never managed to find again. She wasn't the tallest girl on the planet, five foot two in her estimation although I had a feeling she might be taller. Later, several weeks later, as I bent to kiss her during a coffee break, the air coalesced around us and sealed us together. From then on, we were inseparable. Like a couple living in a bubble, kept away from the dangers of the outside world. Yet our immune systems vulnerable due to the fragility of love.

In retrospect, the outside world was of no concern. It was the world inside us which stretched until it tore. Such a tenuous membrane.

During the day she picked up books and put them down again. The second-hand shop where she worked made more money selling valuable first editions online than it did fifty-pence paperbacks to the casual buyer. Whenever I visited it felt like two shops. One front facing, the other hidden. Chloe liked to play on the situation, would tease me as to who she was that day. When I guessed right it was *wounder*. When she tricked me: *bonus*.

I'd pop in during my lunch hour. Pulling my tie askew, buckling my white collar, trying to make myself less of an insurance worker than I was. But as the term *buckling* used mathematically is a bifurcation in static equilibrium, so was my ineffective manifestation of two selves forced and unnatural. The *insurance* me and the *cool boyfriend* me were one and the same. With Chloe, her alternate personas were indeed different. If I hadn't been in love, warning signs would have shot up like defective fireworks, signwriting the sky with the dangers of a potentially split personality.

Not that I saw this at first. Even when Drew brought it to my attention.

Drew was the only girl friend of mine who had never been a girlfriend and who would never be. Duality existed here too. Drew was ostensibly a boy's name, but Drew had been named after Drew Barrymore, the American actress. She liked it immensely, felt that it set her apart. Perhaps for that reason, or perhaps because she was inherently annoying, she believed herself able to offer me relationship advice from both a male and a female perspective.

It was Drew I told first about wanting Chloe to live with me. Even before I told Chloe.

She sucked up coke through her straw and coughed, tiny bubbles like frog spawn populated her nostrils.

"Say what?"

"I want to ask Chloe to live with me."

"Like in, engaged?"

I shrugged. "If that's how she sees it..."

"No, Michael. Not *if that's how she sees it.* You need to be clear right from the start what your intentions are. Because if not, she'll come to a different conclusion than you. I guarantee it."

I propped my elbows on the table. "We're inseparable. We share everything."

"Yeh right, just like you've already shared with her the fact that you want her to move in, instead of running it by me first."

"I'm not running it by you. I'm telling you."

"Whatever." Drew sucked around the bottom of her plastic coke container, made stupid noises. Then smiled. "So, when do I get to meet her?"

I couldn't answer. Truth was, although mine and Drew's friendship was purely platonic, a couple of previous girlfriend's I had never saw it that way. The bubble between myself and Chloe was exclusive. I didn't want anything to come between us.

"What?" Drew looked quizzical. She had a right to be. "Is she crazy, or something?"

I shook my head, smiled. "No, she's not crazy."

"That's what you think," Drew said. "The worst thing is that chicks keep the crazy to themselves when you're falling in love with them, and then when they know you're not going anywhere they let the crazy out."

When I said *Chloe's not like that*—emphatically—I knew that I didn't know.

I told her not to eat cheese before going to bed. Mostly because I didn't like the stale taste of it on her breath come morning, yet also because part of me wanted to believe that it was the cause of the dreams.

"I saw two moons again, Michael. And another apocalypse."

I kissed the top of her head, something that I always did to soothe her. Chloe's eyes were moist. It made her look younger and made me feel protective. Although it was probably more of a comfort to me than it was to her.

She sat up. "I can't take much more of this."

"Don't dream."

She huffed. "You don't know what it's like."

"So tell me what it was like. Share it. A trouble halved, and all that."

With her right hand she tugged at the elastic at the back of her head, struggled her hair through and then reached for her brush.

"You know, Michael, sometimes you can be such an insurance man."

Somewhere inside me, something that I couldn't quite identify but which I knew was crucial to our relationship, developed a hairline crack.

She continued brushing her hair, as though the moment had been forgotten, then she said, "Ok, I'll tell you. If you want the detail."

I raised my hands. "I just thought," I said, leaving the sentence unfinished. I couldn't do anything to help her, could I? Not during the dream. And afterwards it was all just platitudes.

It wounded me that I couldn't take care of her all of the time. That there would always be ways in which she would be untouchable.

"*No,*" she said. "Here is the detail." She moved to sit cross-legged on the bed. She was wearing pink pyjamas with large white spots on them, and I wanted to pull her over and kiss her, but there was no time for that now. She launched into the dream.

"I was in a sort of stable. There were steps just to get into it, and nearby there was a man washing a wall from a ladder.

"The stable then moved, so fast that we couldn't figure out how it was done. Somehow I was in another part of the stable. So I called my mother to have a go, so I could stand outside and see how it worked, but I couldn't.

"There's a plaque on the wall which I can't quite read. I try and take photographs but am unable to and then the plaque changes into a whole other building."

I hear Chloe continue to talk, as if from a distance. I shake my head from side to side. It's like I've got water in my ears, and when that doesn't work I rub my ears with my hands and realise that somehow I'm wearing gloves.

"There was once a huge fire," the man on the ladder says. "Which is why the ceiling is black."

I take a look, but the ceiling isn't black. Just one patch. The man is soaked with water from his bucket.

He takes a step backwards and then he's falling from his ladder and then I'm falling and then I hit the bed and open my eyes and Chloe is watching me and she's neither angry nor surprised that I fell asleep whilst she was telling me the dream. If anything, there's a tentative smile on her face.

"Bonus!"

She shows me the image on the viewfinder. Each of the four seagulls is facing our way, on each of the four wooden stumps.

I show her my photographs. Blurred wings, heads out of shot, crumpled tail feathers adorning scraggy birds' arses.

Chloe laughs. "This is why I'm a better photographer than you."

She's right there. It's as though only she took the course. But I've mentioned this to her before, commented that the best thing on the course was finding each other, and whilst she doesn't disagree I know she's also proud of her photographs and equally pleased that almost all of hers are better than mine.

In front of us, waves muddy the beach. Spume rises like white flies around Christmas cake. Suddenly, I feel hungry.

"Do you want fish 'n' chips?"

"Do you?" She's all eyes, sparkling.

"I dunno. I feel as though I could eat something."

"Then food it shall be," she says, and tugs on my arm and pulls the rest of me along with her as we half-run half-stumble along the sand. Our footsteps uneven, our footprints equally so.

We sit and watch the tide through the misty window of the fish bar.

"Tell me what you said this morning," Chloe says. She feeds herself with her fingers whilst I use the wooden fork.

"About?"

"About dreaming for me."

I don't remember this. And then I do.

"I said I'd dream for you if I could, take the nightmares off your hands."

For a moment I think she's frowning, then I realise a cloud has scudded across the sky and darkened her brow through the window.

"It frightens me," she says. There's an honesty in her voice which frightens *me*.

I pull the skin of my fish with the prongs of the fork. "You do seem prone to the apocalypse," I say. "The two moons, and all that."

She shrugs. "It's just the half of it."

Later, she walks along the sea wall as I hold her hand. We make shadows and photograph them, our bodies like reflected shadows in a house of mirrors.

I look at her shadow: bent, twisted, distorted.

I look at her.

๑

The first night in my apartment she wakes up crying. Deep, heartfelt sobs that even with my arms around her don't show any sign of abating.

Regardless of what she feels, I take the edge of the blanket and wipe the snot from her nose.

"Great," she says. "I've got tissues here." She reaches down by the side of the bed. Some of the tissues have hardened overnight and she laughs and for a moment the fear of the dream lifts and she's herself again.

She's herself again.

I explained it to Drew.

"How do you know," said Drew, "whether the self you want her to be is the self that she really is?"

"You've been watching too many movies," I answer.

"That's you that is." Drew arches her back, suddenly, as though she's been holding her position for far too long. "You want the mystery, but you don't want the mystery."

"That's the mystery," I say, half-heartedly.

"So," Drew pauses. Thinks. "Has this Chloe got a dark underbelly?"

"Pardon?"

"Is it all sweetness and light, honey? I feel you've been skirting around the issue of this skirt."

"You *have* been watching too many movies." I attempt a laugh.

She just turns and looks at me hard and asks if Chloe's let out her craziness yet.

When I wake I'm unsure if Chloe has just dreamt of me or whether I've just dreamt of her.

Her eyes are dry. Our bodies are so close together that I can feel her breathing against my chest. I stop breathing. Start again when she starts, try to hold it for the length her lungs take in air then miscalculate and find she's exhaled before I'm halfway through. I watch the sun penetrate the frayed fibres at the edges of the curtains and wonder why having everything so perfect is so important to me.

"It was like this," Chloe says. "There were the two moons, a heavy sky, like it had been pulled down over our heads like someone trying to pull down a tent. I realise I'm fighting this evil spirit with good thoughts and such. Then suddenly I'm on the floor, having a mergence with good. I'm floating and so high. Reeling in ecstasy. I'm not sure if you're there or have gone or were ever in the dream at all, but I've never been so happy. I feel released. Like a balloon that's been tethered for far too long and has always dreamed of the sky. It doesn't matter if I'll ever come down or if I'll never come down. I'm just up there. Up there. Up. Up. Up.

"Then I awake. I'm alone and all is dark. I know I have failed. That I'm searching for something, yet I have no idea what it is."

Just as Chloe says this I think I have the answer. I sit on the bed counting money: one pence pieces. They all have the same date on but come from different people. 1930. Someone says that is the year someone died.

Then someone hands me a penny in a plastic wallet. I know this will kill the demon. When I try to hand it to Chloe she's no longer there and then I realise I'm dreaming, yet this is her dream, not mine. I want to wake up. I try to wake up. But I don't. And then I do.

Chloe is sitting cross-legged on the bed in her spotty pyjamas. I lean over to kiss her and she turns her head to one side.

Quickly, I try to count her freckles. But there's no point going there.

◎

Only a few weeks later and the dreams are getting worse.

"Fire. Fire in the sky," she says. And when I hold her and comfort her I don't know what to say because I also saw the fire and knew it was me who pulled her out of the dream and that she didn't just simply wake.

◎

"Wounder."

She's sitting on the park bench having kicked off her black Converse to find that the underside of the right one has worn so thin she can almost see the grass on the other side.

"I hate buying new shoes," she says. "I hate breaking them in. I hate breaking anything in."

I try to make light of the holed shoe. "Breaking *anything* in," I say. "Other than shoes, what else have you ever broken in? A horse?"

She stands. Kicks at her shoes with pink and blue stripped socks.

"You," she says. "I've broken in you."

I laugh, then stand as well. I realise my laugh came out cracked. "What's that supposed to mean?"

"Nothing."

"What?"

"Seriously. Nothing. Why does everything have to mean something to you?"

I feel myself becoming defensive. "Because everything means everything," I say. "Even if the meaning is nothing."

She sighs, slips her feet into the Converse. "Sometimes you're all just words. Sometimes I want images."

"And that isn't all just words? What you said?" I said.

She started walking. I reached for her arm as she snatched it away.

"Don't worry," she said. "I'm tired."

"Maybe we should sleep." The sun was high in the sky, burning the backs of our necks. You could hear the buzz of electronics on the boating pond, the air carried a faint trace of petrol.

"Maybe we should dream," Chloe said. She stopped, turned, kissed me full on the lips. "Maybe we should dream."

"Isn't that what we're doing now?"

I wake and then I see the demon. I scream for him to leave. His shape is indistinct, more of a smudge on my retina rather than a physical entity. Fear grips my core. Fuck.

I run for the front door. I have a tiny gold key in my hand with an inscription in my head. I slip the key into the keyhole and it twists by itself.

There's a loud bang. The front of the house pushes out and is on fire. I run to the edge, jump over it and start screaming so hard it hurts my lungs.

Drew comes out of her back garden and says, "The house is on fire."

I'm still screaming and then my sister is there and I hug her and tell her our mother saved us. She had somehow given me the key and the note. Behind me the house is gutted. Then Chloe is on the roof and the house is back to normal. Drew asks why I didn't hear her shouting in the bathroom. She had assumed it was because of the distance, yet I insist in telling her about the demon and then prove it by pulling out the key.

When I try to tell Chloe my dreams she isn't interested.

"It's not a competition," she says. "You know, *your dreams are bigger than my dreams.*"

"Who said it was?"

"Sometimes I get the feeling that's what you want," she says. She looks around my apartment. Her underwear is on the floor, her photographs are pinned around the side of my mirror, hair pulled from her hairbrush lies in a tumbleweed pile in my wastebin. Everything I see reminds me of her and is imbued with the knowledge that we're together and that I can never imagine us not being. The apartment is no longer mine, nor even ours, but it is—simply—*us*.

"This is shit," she says.

"Huh."

"Just this." She sweeps her arm into an arc to take into everything that I just thought was wonderful. "We need to tidy up."

"Maybe," I say. Then realise what I just did again: melded her thoughts with mine. She hadn't trashed my thoughts because she hadn't had them. She didn't inhabit my dreams, I only inhabited hers.

When I wake again, sleep encrusts my eyes to the extent that I can't open them. I can feel Chloe breathing beside me, but can't tell whether she's awake or asleep. Overhead, the two moons shine their light like spotlights, with me at the centre. I reach up my arm and pull at my eyelids, then realise it's not sleep that's embedded in the corners of my lids; they're sewn shut. With one fingertip I trace the ridge of black cotton, in and out of my flesh. But there's no pain, nothing, just the behind-eyelid shine of the moons.

Something hits my face, runs down the side of my cheek.

It's a tear.

"I need you to dream for me," Chloe says, in the voice of the demon.

Then, after what feels like quite some time: "I love you."

A dream enfolds me.

The Quickening

The morning sky was halcyon clear. Autumn. A few leaves still on the trees but most in the gutter. Benedict's bicycle wheels skidded on their slick wetness, his loose chain skipping a ring as he regained purchase. Breaths made visible by the cold floated out of his mouth. His lips were sore from the wind which tore through the city, disturbing bodies that wrapped themselves deeper in coats.

It was the regular journey to work. A small office where after two years he still wasn't sure what he did. Not that this bothered the other employees. They simply left him alone in the corner.

On the brow of a hill Benedict saw someone standing outside what he supposed was their house. The man stood adjacent, on the pavement, on the street side of the gate. He was looking down the road with his hands behind his back. Benedict guessed he was in his fifties. He wore blue jeans and a sweater with red stripes encircling it. His hair pale and thin; but not thinning.

Maybe it was just in the moment that Benedict passed but it seemed he could have been standing there awhile. Benedict's glimpse was but a snapshot, and then he was on the other side of the hill, cycling towards clouds which were tinged pink like candyfloss kisses set against the pale blue of the sky.

Perhaps he would have forgotten about it, save for the following morning: the man looking into the distance, his hands behind his back, wearing the same clothes.

Benedict turned his head as he passed. But the man's expression was inscrutable. He was simply waiting for something. Waiting for someone. Waiting.

At work people were talking about the latest TV shows. Or what they had for dinner. Or what they *would* have for dinner. What they would eat as they watched the latest TV shows.

Benedict unwrapped his sandwiches at lunchtime from their Clingfilm straightjackets. Tinfoil was too noisy an alternative.

A soundtrack accompanied his cycling. His favourite songs complemented each turn of the pedals, worked out a rhythm which he adhered to on the slopes and which spurred him on the flat. On one return journey the sun had already sunk behind the office buildings, refracting light through their multi-windows like a monotone kaleidoscope. Benedict approached an elderly man with a pronounced limp, as if he were walking in time to the music. His right leg dragged behind, the toe of his shoe catching the ground, in a motion of kicking an invisible football. The bend of his knee at a strange angle. Benedict imagined the twist within the trouser. Maybe a sporting accident.

If the steps hadn't followed the music as though in an obscure dance he probably wouldn't have paid it any attention; instead it lodged in his head, with the surety of a metronome's beat.

Back home he brought together the most minimal of ingredients to create a dish he ate with relish as he browsed through the crossword in the free local paper.

The following morning he had a doctor's appointment before work. Just a check-up, he'd been told. This kind of thing happened when people reached a certain age. So he left the house an hour later than usual, again passing the same man with the red circle shirt standing in the same position outside the house. With his arms folded behind his back.

At the doctor's he underwent a full medical examination. Blood tests were taken. *This is routine*, he was told, no doubt nothing to worry about.

It was the *doubt* that played on his mind.

On his return from work he passed the same man with the limp, walking the same beat to a different piece of music.

The weekend came. Benedict drove to the coast and watched the sea come into shore for as long as he could in a freezing wind that reached fingers deep within his jacket and penetrated his skin through to his internal organs.

Occasionally seals were to be found. Black heads, made grey by the pale light on water-drenched fur, would bob in the distance—play tricks with your eyes.

Today there were no seals.

Benedict often thought that when he had a girlfriend he would bring her to this spot—preferably in summer—and show her the seals. But then, in summer, the seals never came.

It was a long drive back. Although much quicker than it would have been on his bicycle.

On the Sunday he boiled potatoes for mash and smothered carrots in gravy. Chicken breasts cooked within tinfoil, sweating in their silvery jackets. Roast potatoes hardened too quickly in the fan-assisted oven. He could never make Yorkshire puddings like his mother had.

Monday he passed the man outside the house. He was tempted to stop. To ask what he was doing. But his bicycle chain slipped a ring and he swerved, straightened, and the impetus was gone.

Nearing work he saw a woman walking uphill with a limp. Her right foot seemed held within her shoe at the wrong angle. As though she had twisted it, and been unable to twist it back. Unlike the limping man, her right leg was stiff with no bend at the knee.

At work, all the talk was of the weekend and what people had or hadn't been up to. There was an office get together which Benedict had missed. Not that it seemed he'd *been* missed.

A week went by as he waited for the blood test results.

On the beach the following Saturday he found a foot inside a shoe. It had been severed at the ankle, just at the shoe's top line, so that if he hadn't looked inside he wouldn't have seen the foot at all. He supposed that it might not be a foot in fact—maybe just a mound of flesh pushed into the shoe with a bit of bone showing. Maybe some butcher's joke. He eased the shoe forwards and backwards over the sand with the tip of his toe. Sometimes it was all too easy to attribute meaning to everything, whereas in fact there was no reasoning to be had.

Over the next few days the incidents repeated. A symphony played inside his head which began with the man standing outside the house, continued with the woman hefting her leg along with the rest of her, and concluded with the man kicking the imaginary football.

His blood test results arrived by post and the letter informed him they were clear.

Even so, the world was off-kilter.

Another person came into play. Another limper. Right leg once again. He tried to recall the shoe on the beach. Wondered which foot it contained; left or right. This limper was younger, possibly mid-twenties. Female. There shouldn't be any reason, he considered, for someone to be limping at her age.

He craved proportion.

Maybe, like an obscure word in a crossword puzzle, it was one of those instances where once something was noticed it seemed to appear everywhere, whereas in fact it had always been there but hadn't needed observation before.

It wasn't long before Benedict's journey to work was populated with hordes of limpers. Yet despite this there was only one man standing outside a house with hands folded behind his back, looking for something which no one could see.

Days at work segued into nights at home. A perpetual routine specific to Benedict; mirroring millions of uninterrupted, specific routines right across the city, right across the country, and maybe right across the globe.

He made variations. Switched from white bread to wholemeal and found a difference in texture rather than taste. Beef spread or chicken spread, it spread all the same. Own Brand products or branded products: only the packaging changed. Maybe his senses were deficient, a recession of the mind. He found himself struggling to differentiate between polar opposites: dead or alive, black or white, good or evil.

Gradually, the constants in his life shifted. No longer was it pointless chatter at work, or the contents of his lunchbox, or the regularity of his Sunday roast. Instead it was the standing man, the limping population. The instances where life folded in on itself, became pocketed, disappeared.

One morning Benedict awoke following the dream of a kangaroo jumping into its own pouch. A finite circle.

His edges were fuzzed.

One Sunday, instead of cooking for himself he drove to the coast and ate in a hotel. The meal was either as good as he could have made it or his usual was just as good as the hotel's roast. He couldn't decide which way around. The waiter served him with a white towel over his arm.

On the way home Benedict had the irresistible urge to urinate. His breathing became laboured. The fringes of cold friezed the car windows with a frost that hadn't shifted despite being late afternoon. He pulled into a lay-by, parked and locked the vehicle. Then he headed into the woods and relieved himself against a tree which might previously have had no human contact.

On the way back to his car he saw a discarded motorcycle helmet.

The visor was down. The glass was tinted. Benedict could not see a face, yet when he picked up the helmet he knew it was heavier than it should have been. The head had been severed at the exact point where the polycarbonate plastic of the helmet ended. A clean cut. He safely assumed this wasn't a butcher's joke. In this instance, there was no coincidence. The helmet had been placed there—with the head—in order to be discovered. In order to gain some significance through him.

Yet the following morning, on his way to work, the man was still standing outside the house, and the same number of limpers populated his journey.

The clues in the crossword became increasingly cryptic. He began to wonder—over a period of days—whether the crossword setter had changed. He was no longer in sync with the answers. They eluded him, sat at the peripheries of his imagination—like *presque vu*—but weren't forthcoming.

He wished he had kept the body parts.

He was being ignored at work.

He took different directions on his journeys, but other than the constancy of the man standing outside the house, the instances of limping occurred whichever route he took. At whatever time of day.

Occasionally Benedict considered telephoning his parents, or his friends.

At night, when the covers were up to his chin, fear crept around the base of his skull. Just at the point where it would need to be severed should he find himself with a motorcycle helmet, a saw, and time on his hands.

More often than not, when Benedict stopped to think, he felt there was a deep anxiety underlying his experiences. The apprehension of being left behind. Of standing at the back of the queue as the rations ran out.

There was something in the air—a quickening—accelerating evolution. This was evident from the vague acquaintances he had, his experiences on the street, with the food products, and in the questions he asked himself.

When he re-read his GP's letter he realised he had been advised to make a second appointment to discuss the result of the blood tests.

Yet it was unnecessary, because as the snow began to fall and he no longer took to cycling to work, and he noticed there were no footprints around the man standing outside the house, and he saw the drag marks that followed the population as they conducted their daily business, he knew that in the twinkling of the once frozen rain that it wouldn't take much to do something to his right foot. Just enough. To fit in. To become prepared like the others.

Flytrap

When Adamson was a boy he imagined a planet.

Days were dreamt in visual soliloquies, quiet monologues. He pieced together a harsh, barren, dangerous world from what he knew of the extremities of conditions on Earth. Volcanoes pepper-potted the surface, craters pock-marked its face. The atmosphere suffocated.

The night sky yielded the products of his imaginings. With head tilted back he gazed through his open casement window, each star a possible creation, each pinprick an aspiration. Adamson scorned the astrological books that his parents bought on special occasions, he didn't want to understand the universe through second-hand knowledge: he wanted to experience it directly.

What made the human race different from the other species was that it sought not only to live within its surroundings, but to adapt them, to expand knowledge beyond necessity, to live outside its means.

Adamson had a special fondness for the brightest light in the night sky. He imagined darkness fell infrequently, that its radiance came from silver-suited occupants who braved the surface and were reflected back into the blackness as a message. He *wanted* this to be a truism. Adamson was lonely on Earth. He felt there were few people like him. If only he had known he was just a typical teenager who would live an average life and see all his dreams shattered, then maybe his perspective would have shifted.

Gareth pinched the fly between his thumb and forefinger. Movement was felt rather than seen, a tremulous vibration resonated within the grooves of his fingerprints and made him want to rub those digits together, to erase the beating of that eloquent heart. Yet instead he maintained the grip, dropped the insect into the jaws of his Venus flytrap.

It bounced once against the plant's interior, then unfolded its squashed wings like an escapologist freeing itself from a sticky straightjacket before rising and buzzing vehemently against the windowpane, catching a breeze and drifting to freedom.

Gareth sighed. He pressed the point of his pencil hard against the paper where he recorded his experiments and made a mark. The fly had been too fast. The trap would only spring when prey had contact with one of the three hair-like trichomes on the upper surface of the terminal lobes. Even then the hair had to be touched twice in quick succession—or two trigger hairs touched within 20 seconds of each other—for it to work. It was a delicate mechanism; also deadly. The trap would shut within a tenth of a second under the right circumstances.

He found the entire process fascinating.

The *Venus* part of the plant's name was a misnomer. It didn't come from Venus. Gareth did, although he didn't know it. Both the planet and the plant had been named after the Roman goddess of love and beauty. The flytrap had been historically known as a *tipitiwitchet*, a possibly oblique reference to its resemblance to female genitalia.

Gareth didn't know enough about female genitalia to make that comparison.

◌

Beth put down her copy of Jack Finney's *The Body Snatchers* and shuddered. She had seen all four movie versions, the black and white classic directed by Don Siegel, the much-lauded remake featuring Donald Sutherland, the passable 1993 version directed by Abel Ferrara, and the execrable *The Invasion* made in 2007; yet it was the book which got under her skin.

There was something about the simplicity: of the idea, of the telling, of the plot, of the invasion. It resonated tiny triggers inside her body; goosebumping the skin, hairs stood to attention. It felt *familiar*, somehow. As though it had already happened and Finney was only setting out the facts for future generations to discover and find truth in it.

She arced herself back on the bed, looked upside-down out the window. The stars were in a reverse hemisphere, but not the opposing hemisphere of the Australasian states. She could still identify the three stars of Orion's belt, the distinctive shape of the Plough, and the bright 'star' that was Venus. She looked for a long time at the planet, until closing her eye she found the afterimage remained on her retina, as though behind her eyelid was a pinhole camera.

She imagined Finney's pods blowing through space and landing on Venus many millions of years ago, sucking the life out of the occupants there, and then leaving it desolate before heading to Earth.

She picked up her phone. It was only just past ten. Laura would be awake. With one push, eleven digits were dialled.

"Hello?"

"It's Beth."

"I know. What do you want?"

"Just tell me something."

"Tell you something...?"

It was a game they had. The recipient of the question would make something up; often nonsense. Beth didn't listen to Laura's words, but she listened to *Laura*. She wondered if she would detect if Laura had been replaced by a being emotionless. If everything that made Laura human remained, or whether it had been subverted. She listened especially to Laura's vowels, because she considered they would be the first to go. Not the staccato consonants, but the resonant vowels.

However Laura's vowels were just as they should be.

Adamson grew older and realised that all planets already existed before he imagined them.

He was only at the centre of his personal solar system.

The sense of isolation remained. It carried through his high school years and into adulthood, where, despite on the surface he hit each of the expected social landmarks at the right time, he found at the age of forty-seven that he could look at his wife and three children and not recognise anything of himself in them.

On nights where the rota dictated that he walk the dog, he took to the hills. The evening sky fought light pollution revealing its majesty. Unleashing the labrador, he looked upwards, basked in the glow. Unlike the constellations which beckoned with promise he knew many of these were dead stars. Their brilliance long extinguished, with the light itself no greater than a memory of it. He fished a cigarette out of his pocket, having taken it from the packet before he left the house, the slender stem had buckled and needed gentle pressure from his fingers to restore its shape.

He saw himself as the bent cigarette.

Venus might be the brightest star in the sky, but he now understood that it wasn't populated by those silver-suited beings of his youth. Atmospheric pressure ninety-two times that of Earth, a temperature that made it the hottest planet in the solar system and air that was 96% carbon dioxide put paid to that. He lit the tip of his cigarette, sucked the smoke into his lungs. For a moment they felt like the hottest part of his body, his chest tightened, he blew out carbon like a world-builder.

What he had looked for in the stars and planets wasn't reflected on the ground. He had barely discovered Earth. So it was that dreams were more than snatched, they were stolen.

The dog barked. Adamson paid it no attention.

Then it yelped.

He drew the cigarette down by half, threw the butt to the ground, and pressed the remainder into the wet soil with the toe of his shoe.

Then he wandered off into the darkness to find his pet.

Gareth found spiders more suitable than flies. Their longer legs triggered the flytrap's mechanism much quicker than something airborne. Beetles also provided sustenance. He would watch as the trap closed, the interlocking lobes becoming prison bars. From experiments he knew smaller insects could escape through the gap, possibly the plant's intention. He imagined the cost of capturing small prey exceeded the benefits of digesting it. But for the larger insects, those that struggled, the trap tightened. Digestion took ten days, after which the trap reopened and Gareth removed the husk of chitin and placed it in a box.

Despite his inexperience he likened the trapping mechanism to a woman. The male an innocent insect, the colourful interior a woman's promise; the trap was life.

Gareth never intended to become trapped.

If Venus were a goddess then she didn't have man's interests at heart.

Still, his tending the plants, his monitoring of their behaviour, his decision how and when to feed: all these elements represented his control. A pyrrhic victory.

Occasionally he dreamt of falling into a giant flytrap, the surface spongy with the texture of a tongue. Knowing it was useless, he would trampoline bounce in an attempt to rise above the closing mesh. Yet it never worked and he knew he would be digested before he starved.

On those occasions he woke and saw the silhouettes of his plants on the windowsill and waited until he could be sure they hadn't moved.

Gareth was no fan of *The Little Shop of Horrors.*

Beth read other books yet always returned to *The Body Snatchers.*

In Finney's work the seed pods drifted through millennia until they reached a planet they might colonise. They affected the guise of the inhabitants although the science itself was sketchy as to how this osmosis might occur. Whatever you do, don't sleep! Unlike the films the book made it clear that the lifespan of these amalgamate creatures was greatly shortened once the transformation had taken place. Five years at the most. Five years to remain in that state—being who you were but not who you were—until disintegration.

Upon which the alien life-form would move on.

She raised this speculation with Laura.

"Tell me something..."

Laura's expression was blank, she began to speak slowly, emotionlessly, until a smile broke her face and she collapsed into giggles.

"Idiot!"

"Scared you, did I?"

"Of course not!"

But wouldn't it be the case, Beth thought, that if an alien were to replace a human they would exhibit the necessary traits required to survive. Finney's book was fiction, and the boundaries set by the book wouldn't occur in reality, would they? If Laura were replaced might she not simply be Laura by any other name.

It was when Beth had these thoughts that she understood her interest had shifted into obsession.

"Boy?"

Adamson never called his Labrador by its given name, because he hadn't named it.

In his mind the name wasn't something suitable to be calling on a hill top whether it was light or dark.

He didn't see it return. A soft form ran around the outside of his right leg and a cold nose nudged the fingers of that hand. Adamson dropped to his knees and held the dog's head within his palms. It didn't shirk, didn't acquiesce to his master's touch. It didn't look frightened or spooked but Adamson knew that it had been.

He clipped the leash, thought about another cigarette. Thought of his wife and children at home in the warmth in front of the television.

There was nothing worth watching.

There was never anything worth watching.

He walked in the direction that the dog had returned. Night hid objects in the darkness. A rock pushed part of one toenail a fraction further under his skin and his swearing formed part of the soundtrack of that instance.

Up ahead a dark shape, possibly a bigger rock, merged into the surrounding blackness like a smudge on a charcoal drawing.

When he reached it the leash he was holding strained and sprang from his fingers. He looked back at the receding golden coat that resembled a blinked out light, and then turned back to the object.

Before he examined it he looked at the sky.

If there was a difference he didn't see it.

He reached out a hand and touched the surface. It wasn't stone.

Gareth knew humans were composite bodies, made of trillions of cells. Some of those cells had been discovered to work independently of the host. Mitochondria, for example, had its own DNA. Yet the differences between life's building blocks were almost infinitesimal. When you really thought about it, life astonished.

Sometimes he ran a fingertip across the tripwires at the heart of the flytrap. When the subterfuge worked, the closed trap took twelve hours to reopen.

He imagined these fake meals must really annoy the plants.

Not that they had feelings.

Feelings were overrated, in any event.

As a boy he had imagined Venus flytraps were linked to the eponymous planet. They certainly appeared to be an alien species.

Not that he could imagine what an alien species might look like.

In a school encyclopaedia he remembered seeing a drawing of a human flanked by two creatures supposedly from planets of differing gravity. One was tall and thin, the other short and fat. The short and fat specimen was marked as a possible inhabitant of Venus.

Should the Venusians exist.

He had doubted the veracity of the speculation without any of the knowledge of what he was.

It would turn out to be correct.

"Tell me something..."

"This is getting boring."

Beth sighed. Laura was becoming less and less the person she thought she knew.

People changed, didn't they? It didn't require an alien visitation for that to occur, they changed naturally. Their emotions fluctuated dependent on external circumstances, their cells degenerated, they were open to other influences and ran with them. What was once funny could be poignant after a disaster. What was a disaster could often become funny. Sometimes only moments after it occurred.

And Laura's distance heightened Beth's wish for change. If only something might happen which would *bond* them again. Best friends forever, that was what their necklaces said. Her mother had told her to grow up, but she *was* fully grown. Wasn't a childhood retreat comforting anyway, like returning to the womb?

Sometimes she wanted a return to the womb.

Sometimes she wanted the whole of humankind to return to the womb.

Laura had got a job in the centre of town. Beth rode the bus with her, to support her on the first day. It had been a while since she had ridden a bus. She looked at the faces of each of the passengers as they boarded, none of them smiling. The bus was an elongated coffin, taking them all to their deaths. Or maybe it was one of Finney's pods, adapted because of its time spent on Earth.

But these passengers had already been changed beyond the people they believed they were going to be in their youth.

Beth didn't want to be one of them.

She wanted to continue in life as she was.

◎

Adamson wasn't sure if it was his hand which was warm or whether it was the object.

He pulled out his mobile phone. There was a torch function which he used when getting behind the TV to change the SCART from the DVD player back to the television. His wife always sighed as he did this, yet she never got up to do it herself. The light ran the battery down quick.

The shape was split in two, resembling a halved coconut. Adamson ran his hand around the outside. Could he describe it as hair? Fur? No, neither. The object's interior was smooth.

He would fit inside it, he realised, with a jolt.

At the same time he knew he *would* step inside it.

He had been going to step inside it all along.

Wistfully he looked back to where the animal had been.

He put down the mobile phone, leaving the light switched on. Then he removed his shoes and socks. Placed his socks inside the shoes. He unbuttoned his belt, undid the button at the top of his jeans, slid them down his legs and stepped out of them. Folded them beside his shoes. This was followed by his jacket, jumper, t-shirt.

Naked, he stepped inside the object and the sides closed around him like a blink of an eye in the blink of an eye.

It was even darker in the pod than it had been outside it. But Adamson knew there would be light.

When the pod re-opened and the body stepped out of it and re-dressed, Adamson's core was already returning to Venus.

◎

Gareth met her at the garden centre. A few years younger, and a few years wiser. She was looking at the sundews.

They weren't common. But after Gareth had expressed his interest in carnivorous plants the owner had bought a few in.

She was tall, with long black hair and a red gash where her lips should be.

He couldn't help himself.

"The sundews, less commonly known by their Latin name of *Drosera*, are so called because of the shiny drops of mucilage at the tip of each tentacle reminiscent of morning dew."

She turned and smiled. "I know," she said. Then she said: "Do you know why you're drawn to the flytraps, Gareth?"

And then she said: "It's all in the name."

Gareth felt as if a button had been pushed in the back of his head. Enlightenment.

"It's time to go," she said. "Time to move on."

She reached for his hand and he took it; half in, half out of himself. He felt like a millstone that grinds against another millstone when there is nothing between them to grind.

He got in her car with barely a passing thought about his.

Her legs were as bare and as light as ice lolly sticks.

Gareth smiled. In the language of humans only a vowel separated a plant from a planet.

And it was time for separation.

◎

Change.

"Change is only natural," Laura said. "Don't you think so, Beth?"

You're becoming something you shouldn't be, thought Beth. *You're dumbing down.*

The bus stopped and they both got off. For a while they walked in silence up the High Street, their long friendship threadbare, coming apart at the seams.

"This is where we part," Laura said, pointing to the large glass façade of the office block where individuality, creativity and independence were culled on a daily basis. She looked excited, but the glint in her eye was temporary; she was in for the long haul.

Beth stepped back. She took a look at her life, speculated her future. Laura's future was not for her. She didn't want the end of the road, with a terraced house and an average husband and average children watching average television programmes in average living rooms.

She wanted the stars.

They air kissed.

Beth turned to walk back towards the bus stop, then stopped.

What if Finney had got it right, but reversed it. What if he knew but couldn't tell people the truth?

In *The Body Snatchers* human's resisted change because they didn't want to lose their core, the essence of what made them human. Their soul. The replacements were identical but emotionless. That single substance, the enigma which separated humans from other life forms—such as plants—was gone. Yet what if the reverse were true. What if humans were in fact empty shells and Venusians came to Earth and entered their bodies and everything which was championed as human intelligence was in fact alien. What if how we defined ourselves wasn't us at all. Or in fact, was us; but we had forgotten where we came from?

She looked up at the stars, couldn't see them because it was daytime. *Silly!*

When she returned her gaze to the street and saw the mundanity there—the people no more than insects—she realised she was right. But that the intelligence was ebbing, humankind—the real, bland, unadventurous, frankly lazy humankind—had begun to dominate.

She sighed.

What she would give for her soul to be repatriated.

What she would give to remain herself again.

Black Lung

For three out of the past seven nights I have dreamt that I live over the bridge.

There's a fairytale quality to that existence, a brushed memory of a fly caught by a careless hand, a smudge of dark beauty. Melancholia infuses my waking head which shower jets won't dispel. Instead wind batters my face on my morning cycle journey, until I arrive at my destination with the sensation of displacement eradicated.

They are filming a documentary on the small island which is barely a few inches from the mainland, and there is friction between the islanders and the mainlanders, although the bridge is hardly a bridge at all, just a scrub of compacted earth, narrow at the point of separation, under which water runs. This realisation grows on me further with each nightly immersion, until I understand that the bridge is purely a state of mind, a condition that the islanders have affected so they are separated from the mainlanders, and it is this affectation which causes the friction and which the documentary makers are so keen to explore.

I sit with sandwiches on a small hillock, tufted grass between my toes. The film crew are spread in a horseshoe a few hundred meters away. Despite the animation of their physical gestures I can hear nothing more than the soft chew of my teeth against the bread and meat of my sandwich. Overhead, something flies.

On each successive waking I found myself unsure if the dream had indeed taken place in the same location, or if I had only *dreamt* that I had previously had the same dream. Or maybe it wasn't upon each successive waking. Maybe that was the point. To be sure I made a short note that I left by the bedside. I didn't record the entirety of the dream, simply *I dreamt I lived over the bridge.*

The wind shakes pussy willow in spun candyfloss streams across the hillock. The air is warm. I call it wind but I recognise a breeze. The filmmakers gesticulate. The scene is idyllic beyond my understanding.

Into this scene enters a figure who cannot possibly belong there.

๑

Rachel finds the notes as she bends from the bed towards the floor searching for wet wipes.

"I dreamt I lived over the bridge?"

My first thought is a startled *you too*, then I realise what she has seen. Even though we have previously slept together her presence suddenly feels like an invasion. I lean across her naked body, squeezing her into the memory-foam mattress like pushing putty into a mould. She holds her arm out, longer than mine, fluttering the paper as though tempting an origami fledgling to fly.

"Just a reminder," I say, although it feels like I am divulging too much.

Breath gasps out of her. "Get off, you're hurting." She arcs her back in emphasis and I roll to one side.

She drops the paper and picks up the wet wipes, pulling one two three out as though white elephants nose to tail. Quickly she splays her legs and wipes me out of her cunt. She folds the wipes carefully and with practised aim hits the centre of the wastepaper basket in a single lob. Then she rolls back over the bed again.

"Where are my cigarettes?"

"Downstairs. Your right hand jacket pocket."

"Oh. Go and get them for me."

"You know I don't want you smoking up here."

She sighs. Swings her legs over the edge of the bed, stands, and pulls on my dressing gown. Barefooted she walks downstairs and a moment later the back door opens, I hear the click of her lighter and she inhales deeply.

The exhaled smoke winds its way upwards and enters the bedroom through the open window.

Ondine carries a handwoven wicker basket filled with unpackaged bread and vegetables. I watch her exit the greengrocers with a pumping heart. She wanders through the documentary makers disconsolately, as though aggrieved they haven't begun filming her. Then she spots me atop the hillock and a smile slips naturally from her mouth as wide as an upturned banana.

I stand and almost run, wrapping my arms around her in a familial affectionate embrace. She stands back, moving a stray group of hairs away from one eye.

"How are you?"

I find my mind split in this dream state. Part enthuses about meeting again, and the other has recognised the impossible. Ondine is here. Ondine is dead.

"I'm good." Is that *my* voice?

She smiles again. "So good to see you."

My eyes slip to the groceries: courgettes, mushrooms, peppers, aubergine. The handle of the basket is hooked over her left arm. Nothing is familiar and yet Ondine is here. She's as real as if she were standing right before me. Which she is.

In the background I see the filmmakers turn their equipment towards us, and I take her right hand and lead her away before they get started. There's something about this land over the bridge which has suddenly turned sinister; not because of Ondine, but of something I cannot specify.

I wake in a gasp. I choose the words carefully, not with a gasp: *in* a gasp. Rachel has her back to me, the covers bunched around her in the moonlight so it appears she has doubled in size. Sunlight is sieved through net curtains. I look to the floor and see the notes.

I dreamt I lived over the bridge.

I pick up my pen and write the sentence out again. Date it.

This is the fourth time I have had the dream in nine nights, but the first time I have dreamt it in Rachel's presence. I want to reach out and hold her, wrap my arms around her sleeping, snoozing, form as though to verify her existence. Instead, I lay on my back and regard the ceiling. The decorator went mad with the aertex in this room. I was forever finding patterns and swirls unknown to me.

The sensation of melancholia I had previously experienced was tinged with a subtle taste of grief. It wasn't entirely unpleasant, containing elements of both what I knew to be true and what I understood to be false. Should Ondine and I have met again, that easy camaraderie of friendship would have been non-existent. Towards the end we hated each other. My ex-wife of five years. My traitor. Even so, I was beginning to wonder if her death had hit harder than I gave her credit for.

The sky darkens and fat raindrops belt against the window, some of them finding a way inside onto the sill. The cactus I have placed there will be glad of it. Turning to my side I see it's barely 6am, yet sleep is out of the question. If I were female—if I were Rachel—I would wake up my sleeping partner. A woman can never allow a man to sleep once she has woken. But my X-chromosome dominates and instead I immerse myself in a book, turning the pages without reading any of the words.

An hour or so later, just as sleep once again presses down on my forehead and I am about to return the book to the shelf, Rachel moans and wakes then falls into a hacking smoker's cough that shakes the bed frame and makes music out of the springs.

She sits up. "Help me." It's more an admonishment than a request. I repeatedly slap her back, aware that the difference is purely psychological, until she stops.

"I need a cigarette." She rubs her eyes with the back of her right hand.

"You need to stop." I pause. "Black lung."

She grimaces. "I told you not to call me that."

"I'll be calling you that long after you're dead."

"What the fuck?"

I agreed. I didn't know where that came from.

⚬

I traverse the bridge. Ondine is already there. She smiles that familiar smile and we engage another warm-hearted hug. There is no romance within us, we are both aware of our pasts and our differences have been forgotten. Yet on the island there is the sensation that neither of us have moved on, that we simply became stationary once we separated and it was only this chance encounter that encouraged us to move again.

If only this were totally true. I can see the changes time has wrought on me, whilst Ondine has reverted to the age at which we first met. She is younger, thinner, full of life and less embittered. She has come to terms with herself and found it agreeable. I can't help notice the liver spots on my hands.

The mainlanders cast furious looks as I crossed the bridge, which seems to have brought the island even closer to them than it was before. Yet they stop, as though the bridge were a fence, glowering before they disperse. The documentary makers wield their cameras as though in combat. At a telegraph pole glimpsed in the corner of my eye I see a white terrier urinating, demarking territory. A tile falls off a nearby house, skittering across the others like a dry-slope skier.

These instances elucidate what I realise I already knew. Ondine is two weeks away from death and she is unaware of it. But I am aware. I am tragically aware. She looks at me and smiles and I remain brutally aware.

Sunlight illuminates one half of a tree whilst the other is in darkness. Children gather around it, in a maypole dance of shadow and light. I watch them spin, unable to look Ondine in the face. The children laugh and then point downwards. An opening has appeared in the ground and initially I think the man who emerges is in blackface. Then I understand he is a coalminer, but not only a coalminer. He is the Engineer.

Ondine is laughing with the children. I recognise the sound, unbroken by sorrow.

Then the Engineer is by my right ear. His whispered voice hauled over the coals.

"It's not a black face you should be frightened of." He places a hand on the white shirt I wasn't aware I was wearing. When he removes it, his fingerprints are as clear as Maori tattoos.

Today Rachel cycles with me although she's unsteady on the bike. We've travelled half my usual distance before I turn to find her stopped, the bike propped against a grassy bank. She sits on the ground in her t-shirt and shorts, legs in a V.

"Give it a rest."

She reaches into her backpack for her cigarettes.

"Like they'll give you breath," I mutter; not sure if my intention is for her to hear me.

I circle, cycle towards her. The sun is hot on my back, but it can't burn away the entropy of my emotions. I am beginning to wonder if the dreams are bleeding into reality because there are just too many of them to be coincidence.

"Take that scowl off your face." She inhales and draws the smoke into lungs which I imagine burn just as bright as the red surrounding the blackened embers at the tip of the cigarette. For me, the direct correlation between smoking and lung disease is obvious. For Rachel not to care is to piss over our relationship and negate her existence as though she is stubbing out her life over death.

Black Lung.

She hates the nickname, but nothing I can say or do makes a blind bit of difference.

"Where are we going, anyway?"

I try to shake off my mood. "I take this route daily. You said you wanted to come."

"I said I wanted to see what you got up to."

I ignore the insinuation. "I continue along this route for another couple of miles, then turn around and come back."

She bent her head, shook it, scattered ash over her once-white trainers.

It was a beautiful route. The area formed what was once a railway cutting through the city. The train tracks long removed, the surface paved in places, left natural in others. Butterflies and dragonflies darted back and forth at all angles. In the summer I would stop and pick blackberries straight off the bush. Squirrels, rabbits, and occasionally a weasel would linger on the path. I looked at Rachel and realised all she saw was distance.

"How does it feel," I asked. "When you inhale?"

She held out the remaining half of the cigarette. "Try it?"

I shook my head. I had never tried it. At school I had always been the one who had rebelled against the rebellious. Whilst it meant I was no different from my parents I knew in my heart I was more the outcast. Living outside the box.

She drew on it again. "It burns," she said. Then she offered it again and when she laughed there was a curious malice in it.

"I am your nemesis," she said.

I wander across the island searching for Ondine.

It has become apparent that the bridge represents the separation of life and death, of the *worlds* of life and death. What is also apparent is that Ondine isn't aware of this. As the dreams continue to commingle, night after night, the two weeks I knew she remained *alive* became foreshortened. I kept the information from her, chatting and reminiscing as though we had all the time in the world. It was like Diana Rigg in *On Her Majesty's Secret Service* all over again. The poignancy was Ondine's helpless unawareness of the certainty of her fall.

Outside of the dream I had met Ondine as an exchange student. She had lodged next door to my parents' house. She told me that her name, Ondine, was a corruption of *Undine*, a water goddess in a folk tale by Friedrich de la Motte Fouqué. In the fairytale novella, Undine marries a knight named Huldebrand in order to gain a soul. The name Undine came from the French word, *Onde*, which meant wave.

The first stages of our relationship had been blissfully ecstatic, with all love's glamour; but we had married too quickly and soon enough the rainbow broke into glass shards which cut our feet with regrets until we could barely remain in the same room without finding fault with the other. Yet still we clung; increasingly in the manner of rotten fruit.

On the island none of this was apparent.

The documentary makers caught up with me, my eyes distracted by Ondine on the horizon.

They wore black suits, white shirts, black ties. When the reporter spoke to me I saw she was no more than an old woman with a brown crocheted shawl hung over her shoulders.

She smiled pleasantly.

"Have you heeded the warning?"

"The warning?"

She placed a hand on my shoulder. The Engineer's imprint was still there and her much smaller hand somehow fitted the template perfectly.

I shook my head, trying to look over her shoulder as Ondine loomed large behind her.

"Your emotions are creating a conduit. You'll have us all in the river if you're not careful."

She lifted her shawl. Underneath, her torso was nothing more than a cartoonist's monochrome drawing. Her internal organs were outlined, but her lungs were shaded grey. As I watched, they turned to black.

Ondine appeared at her side. "I'm..."

The bedsheets were soaked. I thrashed as if they were over my face and I was subject to waterboarding. When I finally disentangled and poured myself fully out of the dream I saw Rachel sitting on the side of the bed with her legs crossed. For a moment I thought I saw the glow of a cigarette, then realised it was a glow in her eyes, then understood it was simply the red recording light on her mobile phone.

"Are you filming me?"

She smiled. "Want to watch it?"

"No." I stood on shaky legs. "I do not want to watch it."

The stairs seemed to buckle with each step. The glare of the light in the bathroom erasing the dream's final residues. I urinated with all the force of frustration.

Before I flushed I sat down on the bowl. My head gripped by hands in a clichéd representation of sorrow. Was I hankering after the sparkling innocence of my first love with my subconscious damning Rachel as an interloper even though the idyllic past was lost and only fleetingly had been? I needed to shake the sensation that the dreams were a series such as a television show. They were subverted memories, no more; night time hallucinations made all the more frightening because they evoked happiness rather than fear: a happiness which I knew couldn't last.

Rachel pushed open the door. "What is it you're doing?"

"Can I sleep round yours tomorrow?"

"Sure thing. Tell me about these dreams."

"I'd rather not."

"Tell me anyway."

I opened my mouth, then saw the lighter she spun between her thumb and index finger. Did Black Lung have a black heart?

She noticed my glance.

"Let me tell you something," she said. "Black lung disease is the common name for Coalworker's Pneumoconiosis. It's caused by a long exposure to coal dust. There's a milder form of the disease, Anthracosis, which is found in some extent in all city dwellers due to air pollution. Pneumoconiosis can develop from Anthracosis and also from the long-term effects of tobacco smoking. But just because I smoke *does not mean* I have or will get black lungs. Dr

Jan Zeldenrust, until 1984 a Dutch pathologist for the Government of Holland once stated in a television interview that he could never see on a pair of lungs if they belonged to a smoker or non-smoker. He said: *I can see clearly the difference between sick and healthy lungs. The only black lungs I've seen are from peat-workers and coal miners, never from smokers.*"

I swallowed slowly. Then I stood and flushed, aware the only exit from the confines of the bathroom was through squeezing past her.

"There's only one way you could know all that," I said.

"And how's that?"

I stood my ground. "You're not who you say you are."

Ondine died throwing herself off a bridge into water so inky black that from the moment she hit it she disappeared and only surfaced two weeks later, bloated and unrecognisable.

The Ondine who sits in front of me sips orange juice through a straw which she believes removes sourness.

She is as young as when we first met, yet today she will die and still doesn't know it.

There's not even the shadow of death about her. Of course, when she died outside of the dream world—in what I am trying to convince myself was real life—she had aged the same way I had. Collecting wrinkles and blemishes and disappointments and heartache as an orienteer might collect clues towards a final destination.

I look into her eyes and that familiar sparkle is there. And then she says, "Oh Joel, where did those twenty years go?"

The sadness inherent in the statement almost kills me.

Yet it is false, we hadn't known each other twenty years.

I wonder if in that statement she has sewn together the present and the past.

Surrounding us the documentary crew relax. They lower the cameras. We're right at the apex of the bridge on the island side, that four inch strip of compacted earth the only barrier between the green grass of the mainland

and that of the island.

Crowded on the mainland side are the mainlanders. On the island: the documentary makers, the children, the Engineer, Ondine and I, are together with the islanders. Our combined weight is almost enough to tip the ground downwards and rent the bridge asunder.

Then Black Lung pushes her way through the crowd of mainlanders, reaches down to the turf on the island side of the bridge, grips it with both hands and pulls it across the gap as though straightening a carpet.

There's a rush of everything at once.

Rachel, what have you done?

Ondine touches my hand lightly, then dives across the gap, transformed into water, into a wave, which settles between the mainland and the island and restores the equilibrium in a second.

Rachel spirals upwards in a vortex, like a twister; twisted.

All that remains of Ondine is a reflection on the water.

The Engineer puts his hand on my shoulder. When he removes it the mark is almost gone.

But not quite.

It could be enough he shrugs.

I awake.

The bed doesn't feel as it should.

I bend over in the semi-darkness and scrawl on a scrap piece of paper: *I dreamt I lived over the bridge.*

On the Beach

When she shows me my rooms, the landlady—who is somehow aware of my profession—tells me how the previous occupant died.

She bustles, skirts furling, hard square heels on the floorboards, an ironed white blouse almost crackling as she walks. *Here*, she says, as she manoeuvres, gesticulating to items which she thinks will be of interest, of necessity. *And here*.

The bathroom door swings open. The suite is 1970s green. Hand basin on a pedestal, toilet with its lid closed, the bath yawning like the mouth of a girl who has eaten gooseberries. Only just enough room for both of us, yet she manages to keep her distance.

In there, she says.

I remark how cold it is.

Exactly, she says. *Exactly*.

After she leaves I slowly unpack my things. The wardrobe has dated considerably. The coathangers permanently attached to the rail. As though I might steal them. Or worse. I hang my jacket and shirts on the rail. Push my leather suitcase into the right right angle. Close the door that squeaks.

I stand on the bed. The top of the wardrobe bears a patina of dust. Someone—maybe a year ago, maybe a few years ago—had stood on this very same bed and written something in that dust. It's indecipherable now, yet the letters show vaguely, a faint delineation of barely thinner particles.

Off the bed I open the wooden veneer drawers of the bedside cabinet. They're lined with newspaper, but it must have been a slow news day. There is nothing of interest.

The edges of the mirror opposite the bed have reacted with the frame. The surface spotted, scarred. I look at my face in the mirror, at my movements. I wonder about all the others who stood here before me and examined their faces. I wonder what they saw.

When people see me they see a disturbed young man. Some say I dived head first into the swimming pool shallow end, others that I fell out of a tree. This isn't a physical deformity referred to, but a mental one. I say I am this way d e l i b e r a t e l y.

Outside the window the snow has melted.

Four weeks ago, the landlady had said, smiling through her thickly-applied lipstick; four weeks ago she had used her spare key to open the door of this room and called for Mr Spence.

He hadn't paid his rent for a week.

On the bed were his jacket, shirt, trousers. On the floor, underpants, socks.

She admitted to rifling through the pockets of his trousers, inside his jacket. *For the rent*, she said; as though this excused it.

Then she went into the bathroom and screamed.

She watches my reaction. Smiles again. She knows I know his rent was paid by the State.

The water had frozen. Ice bit a circle around his neck. His knees poked above the surface. *Like an iceberg*, she said, *with most of him under water*.

She claps her hands, as if to wake me from a reverie, or to break her own spell.

I don't hear the rest.

Now I run a bath. I turn the key in the lock and leave it. I unbutton my shirt, pull my vest off over my head. Unzip my trousers—they fall to the floor like a clown. My underpants follow. As do the socks.

Steam from the bath rises in the air like coalescing wraiths.

The water's surface bears the thick broth of bubble bath. When they melted the ice, she said, air bubbles released a fetid odour.

I look at the bath.

What lies beneath?

Water lies beneath.

I am under water.

The warmth surrounds me like an embrace. I hold my breath. I hold my nose. My eyes close. My ears fill. They fill with water and they fill with sounds.

I can hear movement downstairs, something cooking in the kitchen. A chair scraped back. Faint music on the radio. Or a television. And then I hear something else.

I sit up straight, water gliding off my torso; gasping.

Later, in bed, I wonder how long it would take for the water to have gone cold. For the heating to break. How cold it must be to freeze a bath-full of water. How anyone could sleep long enough for the cold to take hold, to immobilise.

Too long.

I get up. Finger the buttons on my mobile phone. Stand.

The curtains are thin. A gap between them reveals a dark slice of night. I turn off the light. My reflected eye disappears and I see a tree. I turn the light back on and my eye reappears.

Heading into the bathroom I urinate in the toilet then climb into the bath. I kneel, bend my body forwards. Faint traces of water wet my trousers, feed, spread. I put my right ear to the plughole. Listen.

Sounds reverberate.

◎

I am a lifeguard.

Paula doesn't believe me. She laughs. Her voice an accordion of emotions. She lifts both my arms. Lets them fall back to my sides. *There*, she says. *I don't think so.*

Her mouth is a hard thin line when I kiss it.
But I am a lifeguard all the same.

⊙

Jean-Paul Marat, French revolutionary, was murdered in his bath tub on 13th July 1793. Jim Morrison, lead singer with the Doors, died in his bath on 3rd July 1971. George Joseph Smith killed three wives in the bath in 1912, 1913, and 1914. All numbers and names.

In Laurel & Hardy's 1931 short, *Come Clean*, Hardy pulls the plug on Laurel. When Laurel's wife asks of his whereabouts, Hardy replies: *He's gone to the beach.*

I place my ear to the plughole.

The metal circle surrounding the lattice grate provides a cold comfort for my flesh.

I hear...something.

Some nights I wake up shaking believing a spider has crawled into my ear.

Despite the risk, I take it.

Breakfast is communal.

The crockery has a blue and yellow pattern running around the edge. My egg floats ghostly across the plate as my landlady places it in front of me. A sausage, skin hard, nudges it back into place. When she isn't looking, I tilt the plate and soak the grease into my white bread which absorbs it like kitchen towel. Without it, the meal is palatable.

There are three of us here. An old man—older than me—collects toast crumbs in a yellow-grey beard. He also mops the plate with bread, unlike mine which stains my inside jacket pocket he takes small, soggy bites with relish. The other man, possibly my age, eats with his arm half-mooned around the plate, as though he expects me to steal from him. One day, maybe, fancifully, I will.

I watch both of them closely. I was too late for Mr Spence. I was too late for Marat, for Morrison, for many others. But I won't be too late for everybody. Just as I wasn't too late for Paula.

It's Thursday so I head to the job centre. Despite my employment, they won't pay me unless I show.

I hand over my card.

I tilt my head.

What work have I been looking for? I say. *I haven't been looking for work.*

The man before me is new, querulous. He opens his mouth, then an older lady who I recognise nudges his shoulder. *This is the lifeguard*, she says. *The lifeguard needs his money.*

They know me here. I just don't know why they need me to sign on when they understand I'm in employment and will be getting paid anyway.

Once outside I head for the hospital. Wind bites into my jacket, tears pieces off the material, scourges the soft skin on my face. My hands feel as though they are blistering with the effort of holding onto my clothes. Paula liked my hands. *So soft*, she said. *Like a woman's hands.*

I keep them clean, I said.

When I pulled Paula out of the bath the water held a creamy red tincture. I wrenched on her hands and her wrists hung like hinges. Only that they didn't and the memory isn't quite accurate. But certainly as accurate as it should be. As it needs to be.

Her eyes searched the back of her head.

When I kissed her mouth her lips were a thin hard line.

When I pulled her out of the bath I found that she was totally hairless.

In the hospital they tell me that Paula won't see me. I nod. It's been that way for some days. I never know if it's Paula or whether it's the staff, but either way...well, either way is neither way.

I walk back. Buses flash red.

Under the water I open my eyes. There is a bulb in a globe over the bath which seems so far away and yet so close. Like a distant sun.

Water fills my ears with sound. A gentle soothing soughing. Voices are amplified, yet distorted. I hear the memories of those who bathed before. I sense the bodies of those who sank.

Mr Spence is just out of reach. Doesn't he want to be rescued?

Naked, vulnerable, prone.

Dennis Nilsen killed some of his victims in the bath. It's the concave shape which prevents fighting back. The softness of the water. Just relax. Close your eyes. It's like trying to stay awake on the train.

I can never stay awake on the train.

Once, when I missed my stop and had to get off at the next station and then get another train Paula was still waiting for me.

Let's go, she said.

She held my hand and it was softer than hers. She had fingernails like tiny birds' claws, and once when she took them off and showed them to me I nearly fainted.

Her laugh wasn't always soft.

You're half-stupid you are.

But her smile. When she smiled, she always meant it.

We sat on the beach and watched the tide go out. *God's plughole*, she said. I put my hand under her skirt and she left it there.

Later she picked up a shell, held it to my ear, and I started falling.

Back in my room I check to see what my landlady has disturbed, although there isn't any trace of her.

I stand on the bed. Write *Paula* in the wardrobe dust. My finger draws back from the number *4*, from my name. Not yet. Not yet, anyway.

I pull open one of the desk drawers, take out the newspaper. On the underside, the lesser-faded side, I take my ballpoint and circle five separate letters. Then I replace the paper carefully, crease to crack.

The water is warm. I rest my head back, my ears fill with fluid, my nose a periscope. My cock bobs like a flaccid condom in an oil-stained puddle. I am shorter than Mr Spence. My knees are under water.

I wait. Doze.

The water chills. My breath replaces bath-steam. Outside, frost begins to pattern the window, line drawings of trees.

I want to urinate.

I can't do it. I get out, shivering; wrap the damp towel around my body and dry myself sporadically. Still wet, in bed, my form delineates moist against the sheets. I start to shake. Shake and shake. I can't stop shaking.

Some lifeguard I am. Some days I can't save myself.

Next morning the older man doesn't appear for breakfast.

Gone, the landlady winks. As if both she and I know, conspiratorially, what she means.

I have no idea what she means.

The other man, the one the same age as me, also fails to appear.

I get no winks in connection with him.

The landlady tousles my hair as she picks up the empty plate. *Good boy*, she says. Perhaps I should bark. A piece of grease-soaked bread sticks to my inside jacket pocket. When I go out, the smell follows me. Like a curse.

This time, I can see Paula.

They lead me along corridors, passed open wards as revealing as open wounds.

Twin bandages entwine both of Paula's wrists. On one there is a red spot. An ever increasing circle.

It is as though all colour bled out of her.

Her grip is weak, her skin is rough. It's the hours she puts in at the factory.

If she whispers something, then it's no more than *sorry*.

But *sorry* for what? It's my job: the lifeguard. She's my trophy and I tell her so.

Water rises in her eyes as though she swallowed the bath and it found a way back.

Paula, I say.

Like her grip her smile is also weak.

When I kiss her, those lips yield.

I preferred it when they were hard. It's like being sucked into a clam.

◎

I run the water, leave the taps on.

With the water running it's so much easier to hear.

Sounds gurgle, weave, guzzle, disseminate.

I hear them. I hear all of them.

I keep hearing them; as the water reaches the top of the bath without stopping.

Water always finds a way.

I close my eyes.

Footsteps on the stairs. Voices. Shouting.

Mr Spence didn't want to die. It was cramp, as he stood. Cramp bit into his left leg and he went down. Banged his head. Came up and breathed but that was that.

I touch the memory. Release it.

Another successful save. That lifeguard course was worth it.

Then I realise I've forgotten to breathe.

And they're here.

But they can't see me.

Can they see me?

They can't see me.

Nevertheless, whether they can see me or not, I've gone to the beach.

Where Paula draws her name in the sand.

And watches my hand reaching for the stick.

Old Factory Memories

It was only when we were sleep-deprived that we journeyed to Carson's meadow.

We were five: myself, Angelita, Attila, Maciek, and Julie. Claude joined us several months later, his peculiarities rife. Originally these trips were made under the cover of darkness, when the wardens were absent, but they bore night's disadvantages: we couldn't see. Not that there *was* anything to see. But stumbling, falling: those bruises had to be explained come morning.

When we did venture out during the day we tried to convince ourselves that our heightened states led to greater freedoms, although in hindsight I feel the wardens had become disinterested. Technologies overran their minds. There were far too many distractions for them to get involved. So long as we ate, drank, shat properly, and remained presentable to our families then they were content to leave us alone. Those same technologies truncated our families' visits, glazed their expressions when looking at our bruises, and eventually transposed us in their attention altogether.

Life had been different when I was a child. Those glory days of the factories, where product was made by hand, or at the most, with robotic assistance. When product was indeed something you could touch.

That first journey to Carson's meadow came about by accident. Attila had gone wandering. When he returned, two days later, he entered the dining hall puzzled: as though he had only been away for five minutes and had found all the salt shakers replaced. I remember him shuffling over, his hands deep in his cotton jacket pockets. When he sat, an earthy smell replaced the tomato pungency of my soup. He nudged my elbow, removed one of his hands and opened it. On the palm: a tiny piece of brick.

He closed his fist, quickly.

Later, he mouthed.

That night we gathered in Attila's room. Angelita sat on the windowsill, her back against the cool glass, her legs dangling inches from the floor as though she had kicked away a chair. Maciek was slumped on a sofa, his fingers twitching an imaginary guitar. Julie was at the table, a pen in her hand and a blank piece of paper in front of her; creased, like a map. I stood blocking the doorway, my ears attuned to corridor sounds. None of our rooms had doors. They were afraid we might lock ourselves in. We were afraid they might lock themselves out.

Attila removed the brick, passed it around. It wasn't more than an inch in width, under two in length. It had a damp consistency. If you rubbed it gently in your fingers then dust—a fine paste—stained them. Two sides were reddened, the other two grey, as though it was hewn from a larger piece. We all wondered what that piece might be. Touching my fingers with the tip of my tongue the resultant grittiness surprised me. I swallowed, carefully.

"There's more out there," he said. "I know it."

Angelita nodded her head backwards, "Out there?"

"Across the meadow."

We had known it. Of course we had. Each of us had lived our lives within sight of the factory. At least two of us had worked there. But memory is an eraser the older it gets. And we were approaching ancient.

๑

I found my way to Angelita's room. She was suppler than the rest of us, although she still had the accoutrements of old age. A couple of walking sticks lay at angles to the radiator; their stems parallel to each other, at tangents to the groove. In her en-suite a toilet frame assisted with her mobility, and she had a four-wheeled walker with a tray so she could transport her meals to the living room from the small kitchen.

My lips were dry. "What do you think to it?" I said.

She wheezed. "It could be possible. The truth is: he has it."

I nodded. There was no doubting the physicality of the brick, unlike the walls that enclosed us that quivered jelly-like when you got too close.

"When was the last time you were out?" I said.

"Time?" She let the word hang in the air. She was right. There was no need for expansion.

"Attila is talking of this evening."

"Let him talk. Whatever he does, you and I will go."

"And Maciek, Julie?"

"I think they will also come."

"The others?"

"You know they would *never* come. They are not like us."

That was true. I wondered why I had considered it. The home held sixty people. It was easy to count when so few of us moved. We were hardly a flock of birds.

We thought for a moment, our minds working through the mechanics of what we were going to do. For some time, only our rasped breathing broke the silence.

"It won't be the same," I said, finally.

"It doesn't have to be," Angelita answered. "What matters is that it is there."

◎

That first expedition proved inconclusive. The moon illustrated the ground. On the face of it Carson's meadow was an unbroken expanse of grass, but whilst there was uniformity across the tip of each blade, the roots dug into the earth unevenly. Maciek was the first to drop. For a moment, in the dull light, he couldn't find himself. Attila swished ahead with his stick. "It was here," he kept saying, "I was sure it was here."

What was clear was that the meadow wasn't always as it seemed to be. On our second journey Julie claimed to have found something that none of us could see. It was only when we returned to the home that it became clear—or rather, opaque. A four-inch shard of glass, green-stained and sharp. "I told you," she said excited. "I told you it was there."

We took turns describing what we had seen. All our descriptions matched, other than Julie's. But this was merely in the details. Her deviation was finding the glass.

So we examined the facts, took the investigation beyond the external and towards the internal. It was then that we discovered Julie's medication had ceased two days beforehand and she was finding it difficult to sleep. She was self-medicating, she said, but kept forgetting to inform the staff that she was low. Maciek nodded his head, thoughtfully:

"Chronic sleep-restricted states cause tiredness, clumsiness, a discordance between speech and action; but perversely there are also some cases where sleep deprivation leads to increased energy, alertness and enhanced moods. Sleep deprivation has been used as a treatment for depression."

Attila nodded. "I had been experimenting, too."

It was difficult to argue the point, nevertheless that piece of glass joined the artefact of brick which—for safety's sake—we kept balled in the foot of one of Attila's surgical stockings.

And we tried again, a few evening's later. The medication we had been given to sleep, to ensure our nights were trouble free, that our days were spent awake and active, we palmed and put to one side. We fought against natural tiredness, relocated ourselves to Angelita's room once lights were out, and jostled, sometimes even kicked each other when in the combined darkness we felt one of us slip away.

Only then did we feel capable of revisiting Carson's meadow.

That night—the night of our revelation—we huddled together as a group, hoping should the wardens glimpse us we would appear as one mass of shadow rather than five separate escapees. Carson's meadow was vibrant in moonlight—although it was impossible to determine if we were seeing it with our re-wired brains or if the circumstances were simply favourable. Maciek had suggested one of us continue with medication, so the journey could be considered a controlled experiment. But he didn't volunteer for that, and neither did the rest of us.

This time, treasures were in abundance. Not only was the surface uneven, it was stumbling ground. And with the accumulation of objects, with the sensory perception our feet pulled from the walk of the earth, I began to see the factory build itself before us.

I remember reaching out for Angelita's arm, almost toppling her in my suddenness.

"I know," she said. "I see it too."

◌

We hit peaks and troughs. Some days we had to sleep. Just at the point that the factory seemed complete it would crumble and turn to rubble before our eyes. For a month we couldn't synchronise our conditions. Maciek developed a urinary tract infection which—he claimed—caused the building to be plugged with electricity. Where lights illuminated each of us in our own separate rectangles on the grass of the meadow, replaced our yellow wan faces with those of youth. He could speak of nothing else for days, then became a silent member of the group, his expectations no longer matched in whichever reality he resided.

That moment when we understood the wardens would not prevent us venturing outside during the day was the closest we came to Maciek's revelation. Of course, we were not confined indoors. The ceilings would roll back in good weather, although were not always as fast to replace when it rained, and there was a communal garden where residents might throw bread to ducks or bake in deckchairs until they were remembered. I recall the five of us, with our various contraptions, shuffling out of the home—all our infirmities evident under the senseless sun. We were a pathetic bunch. Even Angelita, in this light, could not be saved from her years. My eyes ached with looking at her.

Sleep-deprivation confused my memory. That was my catalyst. I would develop a headache at the base of my skull, a gentle pressure. My eyes could not focus. My brain less so. But it was easier to collect rubble during daylight. Instead of falling over it, instead of running the risk of twisted ankles, painful insteps, you just looked down and saw it within the grass. Later, Julie brought her hand-grabber along with us. By flexing her fingers she was able to prevent us from bending down. I would have gladly made use of it myself, if it wasn't for the arthritis which restricted my movements. The most I could do was crouch and struggle.

We were running out of places to put it all.

One day I entered Attila's room to discover our finds were spread out across his floor. He sat, cross-legged, building a structure. It was rudimentary, incomplete, but I knew it was coming along. When he looked up I saw him smile as if for the first time.

It was then that I realised this wasn't because he had created some form of art, but because of his posture. He was pain free.

Over a year into our discovery, Claude arrived.

He was gaunt. Had once been over six foot tall. Even in his current state he dwarfed Angelita. A shock of white hair gave him a permanently reanimated look. He always wore a yellow handkerchief in his jacket pocket. A square which was never unpleated.

Perhaps even despite his striking appearance he would have faded into nothingness if Claude hadn't been assigned the room next to Attila's. We passed it one evening, Claude standing against the window as if he and the glass were opposable magnets. We halted, somehow entranced. I hadn't slept more than six hours in three days and my mind was bobbing like a balloon a couple of inches above the top of my head.

Claude picked up on this. He turned and snarled.

I stood, faced him off. Then he crumpled and we abandoned our mission. Attila stayed with him whilst the warden arrived.

Later, Attila said: "He suffers from double vision and progressive memory loss. He becomes easily disorientated, overly paranoid and confused. I overheard a conversation with his family. He has fatal familial insomnia. We should ask him to join us. He lives in the moment. That's what his daughter said, as though it were an aberration."

We weren't immediately convinced. Attila—who coveted the objects—was too enthusiastic. We wanted reason. Julie wanted to remain as she was, the increase in the dimensions of the factory had started to disturb her. Maciek also was seeking something none of us had ever seen. But it was Angelita who put her finger on it:

"None of us are getting any younger. We have to consider both the fragility of our bodies and that of our minds. Something is happening to us: we can't go back. If we delay too long then one member of this group will be lost; then another; then another. I don't want to be left with only memories of *us*."

I nodded. I made a speech about not wishing to wade through fields of grass, bending for femurs, molars, strips of flower-patterned dresses, or the frayed shoelaces which Attila always wore. We needed to enter the factory before death entered us.

I was to be their spokesman.

I chose what I considered to be the best indicator of our finds: a metal cog, coin-size. Not that I had seen a coin for some years. The outside edges were double-serrated: a row of teeth behind a row of teeth. None of it could have been recently fabricated. I hoped Claude would appreciate that fact.

I sat on a wooden chair, my elbow resting on his table where the remains of vegetable soup resettled after his meal like the layers of a river after a particularly intrusive storm. "Well?"

He turned it in his fingertips. "It's authentic."

There was a pause, as if he were conjuring what I might know with what he wanted to say.

"Did you find it on the meadow?"

I nodded.

He muttered something indistinct. I caught the words *man* and *forest*. Then he rose from his sitting position to full-height. "I could be your guide."

Given Claude's health our first journey as six was under cover of darkness. Claude's mobility was exceptional compared to ours, however his mental state had deteriorated even in the few months since his first appearance. Day time hallucinations and panic attacks had become noticeable. Oftentimes his doorway could not be breached. However, as night fell he seemed soothed by its closeness. His concentration of wardens lapsed.

He led us towards Carson's meadow as if he already knew the way. We stood still in a gentle breeze. Together we had already created the foundations, our collective unconscious made visible. Within seconds Claude added windows, a roof. He confirmed his visions verbally, and they appeared like the lines on an Etch-A-Sketch. I heard Attila gasp. The others were silent. To see a useful building: Angelita came close to tears.

We spent four months improving the detail. Julie chose a wall to add decals, conservative graffiti. Maciek concentrated on the upper floors, their windows billowing light and shadow. Angelita contributed noise, action. I built the chimneys, tall, white structures like a pair of opposing brackets or the figures of shapely maidens.

Claude was the cipher through which this was possible. His insomnia was inherent—a disease—unlike ours which we affected through a lack of medication and passion. He rapidly lost weight, and on some days was unresponsive and mute. On those days we could do nothing at all, and I became terrified that he would slip into the final stages of his disease, not unlike dementia, which would lead to his death.

Yet it was not Claude that almost jeopardised the project just as he enhanced it, but Julie.

I saw the bottle-end first, a trapped piece of history in her grandson's grasp.

The smile on Julie's face was fake, drawn by a child. It had no bearing to her mental state, or rather her mental state had no bearing to her.

I watched as the child turned it over in his hand, curious about the physicality. His parents sat side by side in the common room, their eyes darting towards Julie then sliding away. Mouths half-opening, then closing. After a few minutes they became engrossed in their own technologies, their heads in their laps, as if they had nodded off mid-afternoon after a meal of meat and gravy.

"What you got there son?"

I placed my stick at an angle, blocking the child's circular route. He held the glass aloft. I remembered airplanes. But he knew it was wrong. *Something pretty*, he finally said.

"May I see it?"

My heart was scrabbling in my chest, my breathing restricted. I would fall, I knew, if he didn't give it to me quickly.

He was a bright boy. I couldn't reveal my desperation. I saw one of the wardens glance across. It was too dangerous. I ruffled the boy's hair. "It doesn't matter," I said.

Before I could move he slipped it into my pocket.

For the remainder of the afternoon he stole me glances, on those few occasions that he looked up from his technology. I wondered if I had turned a key. If there was a way out from what humanity had created. I wondered if I really knew anything at all.

⍜

Attila checked Claude's pupils.

"They're like pinpoints," he said. He looked at his hands. They had come away from Claude slicked with sweat.

Claude had spent the previous evening doubled up with the pain of constipation. I could tell our days were numbered. Attila shuddered in his room next door as Claude's bowels were manually excavated. The following night he said: "It's now or never."

Claude appeared stuck in a state of pre-limbo sleep. Whilst awake his limbs moved repeatedly, as if he were dreaming.

Maciek became impatient. "Let's get him out of here." He paced.

Julie had no memory of passing the bottle-end. Her time was close.

Angelita and Attila were the most lucid. I could feel my own edges blurring, as if the descent into the abyss were being prepared for my fall like coastal erosion.

Then, as though pulling myself out of sleep, I woke.

We entered Carson's meadow in various states of mind. Summer was leaving. The breeze had an edge to it. The ground was harder, pitted. Angelita fell heavily. I watched Attila help her rise with no trace of bitterness. The factory dominated the skyline. It commanded my view. I tried to imagine the time I believed I had spent inside, when the meadow was tarmac and white lines delineated the rectangular positions of parking spaces. Where the foyer was corporate and the interior working class. I could smell the grease they used on the cogs, a rich memory; a sensory awakening.

We stood in a line, aligned. I looked across to my colleagues. I remembered that tiny piece of brick crumbling in my hands. Self-consciously I put my fingers to my tongue.

Our walking aids fell to the grass. Our bodies, I am not so sure.

Dizzy Land

It was California. But it wasn't California.

The sands stretched into the distance, flat and wet as drying cement. They reached the sea slick. Gulls arced upwards then fell like confetti at a poor man's wedding. Close to the roadside two children stood with yellow plastic buckets and spades, wondering whether they should venture onto sand which would suck at their feet as though it owned them. Nearby shops were boarded up, graffiti adorned the shutters, crenulated messages.

Hunter took it all in. It wasn't much. But it was all he could afford.

For years he had worked as a showman at travelling fairs. Packing up equipment, journeying, unpacking it amid faulty lightbulbs and garishly-painted signs promising the thrills and spills of yesterday, operating and supervising rides, packing it away again, travelling, never finding a space to rest or relax. Now it would be different. Now he was here. California or no California.

On the Norfolk coast, California owed its name to the discovery of 16th century gold coins on the beach in 1848, at a time when the California gold rush in the Americas had captured the world. But California Sands was no more than a second-rate grubby series of shacks whose name belied its origins and where if it wasn't for the sea it would hold no attraction at all. Yet, for Hunter, it was the chance for a new beginning. It could be the dawn of another age altogether.

For now, though, he turned his back on the sea and rolled up his plans for the amusement park into a long thin tube. Resisting the urge to gaze through them like a telescope, he held them with a firm hand against the increasing wind and made his way back to his car.

"We need the development," his landlady said, as she slopped a hefty English breakfast in front of him. "Good on you. Good on you."

Hunter shrugged and cut into a fried egg which burst like the eyeball in *Un Chien Andalou*. A thin line of ketchup bloodied his plate, turned the yellow orange.

"You think it will catch on, like?"

He forked the egg into his mouth, ignoring the question. He knew what she wanted. The trade that Yarmouth's *Pleasure Beach* brought. But further up the coast California Sands was no Yarmouth. Despite that, it was obvious she would be happy with the result. *Dizzy Land*: a series of permanent attractions of fairground rides. Waltzers, Carousels, Scramblers, Orbiters, and of course, his personal favourite: The Rotor ride.

There weren't a large number of Rotor rides in existence anymore. The simplicity of it and the urge to create better and faster rides had created a lack of appeal. Yet for Hunter the Rotor was everything. It was the ride he had manned at every fun fair he travelled with over the past twenty years. For him, the simplicity *was* the appeal. A large, upright barrel, rotated at 33 revolutions a minute—just like an old long-playing record. The rotation of the barrel creating a centrifugal force equivalent to 3g. Then, once the barrel attained full speed, the floor was retracted, leaving the riders stuck to the wall of the drum. It had the added benefit of attracting paying customers who only wanted to watch rather than ride, with a wall running along the outside from which a viewing platform looked over the centre. As far as Hunter was concerned, it was a money maker.

With the tines of his fork pushed into the white, he spun his remaining egg around on the plate. Flecks of oil tarnished the dining room floor. The landlady was in the kitchen, whistling a tune Hunter didn't recognise. It was always a tune he didn't recognise.

Local council planners had treated his proposal with respect. Funding was desperately required in these seaside towns with their seasonal employment and in-bred inhabitants. If he had wanted the plans rushed through he couldn't have had a faster service. The coast here was as flat and unappealing as an undercooked pancake. There was none of the gaudy glitz of Yarmouth, nor the interesting will-it-or-wont-it-fall-into-the-sea erosion at Happisburgh. Nothing here apart from the shacks and a bit of sea which was only warm in November. If there ever was to be a *Dizzy Land*, then California Sands was the cheapest and most needy location.

Hunter decided he had finished his breakfast and returned to his room.

He turned the key in the lock, lay on the bed wearing his suit that had seen better days, and tried not to think of Rebecca.

◎

Simon paused and shielded his eyes against the heat of the sun.

"I can't see to paint, mate."

"Hey?" Hunter shouted back, holding the foot of the ladder.

"I said, I can't see to paint, the sun's too bright."

Hunter sighed. There were always issues, always problems. Yet Simon was one of the best fairground painters he knew. The colours were just right, like the enamel paint you would use for toy planes or soldiers in your youth. Ultra-rich. They hung like there was a curve to them. And there were plenty of curves in the girls that adorned the side of the Rotor ride. Simon had depicted them perfectly, pressed against the inside wall, a skirt rising here and there. One could have been Marilyn Monroe, with the outstretched arm of a James Dean lookalike stretching out—unable to touch her. Jeans positively bulged with paint, shirt sleeves barely concealed muscle, and halter tops strained with mounds of flesh. Fun fairs and the promise of something illicit always went hand in hand, despite the *Hook-A-Duck* attractions for the little ones. It was under darkened night skies, lit like Christmas trees, that teenagers found their homes, their soulplaces. And Hunter knew it like no one else. Because Hunter felt like he had been there right from the start.

He had been born with a hole in his heart, a defect in the wall of two of his chambers. Throughout his childhood his parents had repeatedly told him not to waste his life because he was lucky to have one. Consequently, as soon as he was old enough, he left home for the attractions of the fun fair.

It was there he met Rebecca and sustained the second hole in his heart.

The ladder shook. Simon was coming down.

"I can't work from this side right now, I'm moving to the shade. Will start at the bottom. You coming?"

Hunter shook his head. "You're alright by yourself. Don't need my supervision."

"Tell me about it." Simon carted his stuff over to the opposite side of the ride.

Hunter pushed his hands into his pockets. Wearing the suit was incredibly uncomfortable, but necessary, in his mind. He picked his yellow hard hat off the floor and wandered around the remaining rides which were still in production: the Helter Skelter, Wavewings and the Carousel. Nothing too fancy or modern. This would be a place where parents could bring their kids for a nostalgia trip. That was okay with Hunter. When you reached a certain age it was all nostalgia anyway.

Spring had come early and hot. It was just a few weeks until Easter yet already it felt like the summer had rode the coast forever. When it was this hot, Hunter couldn't ever imagine it being cold. Yet that was the same as *love*—wasn't it, the word sticking in the back of his throat even as thought. But just like the wind, love blew hot and cold.

Although it was barely possible for him to dig his hands any deeper into his pockets, he did so, clenched them, and walked on.

⦾

Out of season, fairgrounds were a wiped smile from a clown's face.

It was as though the sun oiled them, supplied the electricity, the motorised purr.

In winter, like desultory toys lying in dust in a dead child's nursery where the parents wanted to preserve only memories, the machines were lifeless, deadbeat. The cold and the wind bit into the wooden surfaces, however hard and tight you covered them with tarp. They might well be abandoned, part of a nuclear landscape; yet give them a bit of sun and they were reanimated, better than zombies. Just as good as they always were.

Hunter and Rebecca's relationship similarly fluctuated. From the depths of the dark to the bright of the light. And once in one the other could never be imagined. Hunter might cut his torso with a knife only for it to heal without a blemish. That was his analogy. However frequent the cuts, the skin smoothed over. That was how he expected it would always be with Rebecca.

Once the contractors left, just a week before opening, with all the paint finished and as sparkly as a glitter ball, with everything new and untouched and as yet untainted by staff Hunter knew he would have to employ, he decided to spend one evening under the stars with his dream.

The sun had gone down leaving a pale residue of warmth. Whereas spring might be early, it left early too. Some mornings the grass bore a speckle of frost, as though it had witnessed the overnight migration of thousands of snails. Hunter's suit was thin and cheap yet as he wandered around the deserted attractions something swelled inside him and kept him warm. He ran his hand across their smooth surfaces, smelt the upholstered padding of the Waltzers, heard the creak of the traditional wooden platforms, freshly varnished. When he approached the Rotor, the painted figures seemed to spin and turn, their beautiful smiling faces tinged with acceptable fear and excitement might have been alive. Hunter found his own face smiling. It could have been a crack in cement. And thinking of it, he almost laughed.

Maybe it was this. Maybe it was a memory of him pressed against Rebecca in a kiss as the floor retracted under their feet, maybe it was the force of his back to the wall, or maybe it was simple curiosity. Whatever it was, he wanted the ride.

It had to be simple for the ride's operators, who through Council planning regulations he was required to employ locally. Rural regeneration projects came with a lot of money and they bolstered his funds. He couldn't argue, but given the nature of the locals he had arranged for the ride mechanisms to run automatic if necessary. A button to start the ride, and then on a timer to finish it. If necessary, the timer could start the ride too.

Hunter opened the side door of the Rotor and entered the polished wood of the barrel.

When he was young, there was a fixed fairground Helter Skelter that culminated in a polished wooden bowl rather than just the foot of the chute. Something in that wooden bowl, the ride at the end of the ride, appealed; the dark polish of the surface. The interior of the Rotor was similar. The smoothness of the wooden planks, fitted together as though they had grown together. For Hunter, something that was so rough which could be so smooth became a metaphor for himself. Rebecca saw it when she wanted to. If only it had been more often.

He positioned his back against the wall, his feet touching the retractable floor. Held his breath.

If there was a click he didn't hear it, then the sides of the Rotor began to turn.

In the pit of his stomach, trepidation such as that found when a roller coaster moves away from the platform, or a plane begins its taxi down the runway, tensioned inside him. The point of departure. The point of no return.

He felt sick.

The Rotor turned faster, gained momentum, Hunter could feel the force pushing him back against the wall. The skin of his face fluttered, he smiled and the sides of his lips pulled back in a rictus grin. He tried to move his fingers, but other than a slightly raised knuckle they were pinned in place like a butterfly on a green velvet board.

Under his feet, the floor began to pull away.

Hunter had test run the rides a week previous. For two days the funfair had crawled with Health and Safety Executives, carrying their requisite clipboards and pens. So he knew there was nothing wrong with the ride, even as the gaping maw which opened beneath him suggested otherwise. He tried to look down but his head was pushed back to the wall just as surely as if it were held there. Through squinting his eyes, though, the depth of the drop confounded him. Wet brick, smeared with greenish moss, fell away beneath his feet like a recently discovered medieval well. And surely in the corners of his vision something moved in the darkness, something circling, almost noticeable, yet not quite.

The timer ran around and the floor returned. At the end of the cycle gravity regained a hold on Hunter's body and he began to slide slowly down the wall. As the ride stopped he collapsed, gasping, his heart palpitating fast. He lay face down, pressed against the surface of the floor, fearful of what lay beneath.

"Not long now, Mr Hunter. Not long now."

He would have changed digs but there were few guesthouses close to Dizzy Land and despite meal time interrogation his landlady didn't seem too concerned by his comings and goings. She had certainly turned a blind eye as he had entered this morning, his suit in disarray, with cold beads of sweat populating his forehead like bubblewrap.

He pushed his eggs around his plate. Cut into a sausage. Something small, white, and hard lay at its centre. He spooned half a plum tomato into his mouth and a flavour-burst exploded before he could gag. He swallowed it down. Breathed slowly. Ate again.

"Under a week," he mumbled.

"Under a week," she parroted, as though she were repeating the fact of a find of gold, more than 150 years ago. "Under a week."

Hunter finished his breakfast, to his own surprise, and returned to his room where he slowly removed his suit and underclothes and stood underneath the lukewarm shower, his eyes closed against the half-hearted jets that pummelled his face.

He had awoken on the floor of the Rotor just as it was getting light. The sun illuminated a semi-circle interior. He had stood, stiffly, looked around without comprehension. And then he had comprehended, without understanding.

There was no one he could share this with.

He turned off the shower, felt the water find its way down his body and into the plughole.

The drop wasn't possible. Two feet maximum. The night had played tricks with his eyes. Whilst he didn't believe he was stressed about the opening of the park, such pressures were inevitable. It had just been a glimpse, nothing more, a play of shadows.

He continued to tell himself this as he dried wet skin with a towel and his breakfast threatened to return outside of his body.

An hour later and he was interviewing the locals. The few who could string a decent sentence in English he assigned to the rides. Most of them were Polish. He found himself shrugging, wondering whether these employments would satisfy the local regeneration project and found himself past caring. Those who were English who attended the interviews weren't even fit to clean Dizzy Land's toilets.

Another hour later and Hunter found himself standing on the observation platform as Feliks operated the controls. The floor opened to reveal the dark canvas that masked the grass underneath. Nothing unusual there. Hunter pulled out his handkerchief and rubbed the sweat away from the base of his neck. The spinning barrel reflected in his eyes and suddenly he pressed the handkerchief to his mouth, contained his breakfast once again, and vowed to have croissants in future, should his landlady allow it.

"Is ok?"

"Is ok," he shouted back, mesmerised by the mechanism as the floor returned with the precision of a musical box.

Come darkness, he stood before the Rotor ride again.

Rebecca had slipped her hand into his in the Tunnel of Love. It was corny as hell, but being teenagers and expecting the corn they ate it.

She operated the Tea-Cups, and whenever he saw her open and close their two-tone sides to allow the younger children access he imagined a future in which he left for work and she opened and closed the door of their home, waving as children—their children—clung to her legs. He would vault the white picket fence at the end of their property and she would laugh and smile and he would retain her beauty imprinted on his retina until he returned from work and she would kiss him just as she had done at the top of the roller coaster. Just before it had descended and they had screamed and his one-hole heart felt it would burst from the touch of her tongue.

Hunter rubbed his hands over his eyes. Pressed himself to the wall of the Rotor. Pushed against the back of his cranium was a piece of foam he had picked up outside an upholsterers, waiting for a rubbish collection. It angled his head downwards, counteracting the centrifugal force. As the Rotor began to turn on its timer Hunter's breath once again caught in his mouth. Time slowed. He released the breath and it started again. The barrel began to turn.

This time, as the floor fell back, the true depths revealed themselves to him.

Stretching as far as the eye could see the brick walls of the well tunnelled directly underneath him. Above, the moon illuminated enough to see that there was more to be illuminated. Shadows flickered within the well, winged demons which—once they caught sight of him—began to circle ever closer to the top. If they had lips Hunter was sure they would have licked them. He watched with an abhorrent fascination. A replay of an out of body experience which he knew couldn't be true just as he knew he was experiencing it.

Then, just as the demons were halfway up the well, the floor began to retract and gravity reasserted itself and his feet slid back down the side of the wall until he was resting in safety on the ground.

There was an ache in both the holes of his heart.

He determined to leave immediately, but the entrance door could have been a million miles away.

So he remained standing. Looking at anything other than the floor and the truth it contained.

◌

His landlady sighed as she collected his plate of half-eaten fully-buttered croissants.

"You need to keep your strength up, Mr Hunter. Big day tomorrow."

Hunter shrugged. He no longer thought of Dizzy Land as his future. Whereas he had struggled and managed to keep going over the past few days, ensuring everything was in place for the opening, and even conducting interviews with the local newspapers and radio station, it was all artifice. Just as the floor of the Rotor was a pretence at what really lay beneath. Just as his relationship with Rebecca had turned to pretence. More winters than summers, more autumns than springs.

"This can't go on," she said. From her position on the floor she looked so small, so tiny. The bruise on her lip purple, as though a blueberry were growing under the skin.

Hunter fell to his knees but she flinched, as though he remained looming over her. He opened his mouth and nothing came out. Words eaten by a jealousy which he held no right to, which nothing substantiated apart from the terror of his imagination and the fear of losing everything that he had.

Hunter had spent five nights staring into the abyss. On one occasion, the mechanism had blipped and he was sure he would have fallen if it were not for the plastic guard which protected his feet from the drop. He didn't know whether to thank the accident at the Cajun Cliffhanger in the States which legislated the redesign over ten years previously, but it saved his feet being crushed by the late returning floor as he had begun to slide down the wall. The demons had rested less than two feet into the darkness, grinning, beckoning, but not moving further forwards.

Maybe there is an invisible skin between their world and mine, Hunter had thought. But in reality he knew there was no skin. All there had been was choice.

Travelling fun fairs operated like the solar system. No two planets, no two fairs, were ever in the same place at any one time. Once Rebecca left, he had heard she was travelling the east coast as he travelled the west, that she the north whilst he peddled the south. After a while, several years in fact, she disappeared completely. Right now she was probably closing a door with a smile waving at a man who was not Hunter, with other non-Hunters clutching her legs with love.

The Polish could run the fair without him.

He watched his landlady walk away with his half-eaten food, tutting softly to herself.

Another half, another hole.

His heart wouldn't take it.

That night, the final night before the big day, Hunter set the timer on a loop.

He pressed his back against the wall, held his breath as the Rotor began to turn, as the polished sides of the barrel spun in front of his vision, and as the floor fell away and the demons watched and waited, feeding on his failure at the pinnacle of a success that he would never be able to share, he closed his eyes and imagined what could have been, his body fixed like a question mark over the drop.

The Opaque District

Jay knew things were getting bad when he saw there were queues to join the queues.

He hadn't watched television for some time. The news held so many cuts it seemed like the government was falling through brambles, although Jay held a suspicion that the government's stance was akin to Brer Rabbit pleading not to be thrown into the briar patch. The government could handle the cuts, alright. Its job was to pass them onto everyone else.

Pale sunshine had filtered through his stained window that morning. The paucity of the light seemed reflected by the economy, as if everything, the entire reality of the world, had been stripped back to basics.

He had heated some water in a saucepan on a hob that had seen better days, then felt around in the glow of the flame for yesterday's tea bag. He remembered the luxury of steeping a bag for a full two minutes, before adding a healthy drop of milk and three unhealthy spoons of sugar. Now he had grown used to the tea from a bag he barely allowed to dampen, and milk and sugar were sweet reminders of times past.

It had happened quickly. The world banks had called in their debts. Then everything had folded like a birdcage in a magician's trick. Provisions were rationed then fought over. Jay could remember seeing his first ever street fight. It couldn't have been more than two months ago, although it now seemed folklore. The man had been outnumbered. His grocery bag had split, and the newspaper he had stuffed around the edges to conceal the contents flew out at the sides like Marilyn Monroe's skirt. Five tins—corned beef, peas, carrots, a Fray Bentos pie, and something Jay couldn't quite determine—hit the ground and rolled, their bent sides describing a disjointed arc. They were pounced on by three men, and when the owner had raised the quietest of objections he found himself lying on the ground with a broken nose scrabbling in the recent blood for his missing teeth. Jay could only speculate on what he intended to do with them.

Scuffles had broken into looting, looting into shooting. That two month burst of panic had spread like shotgun pellets until the only things which were left were those at the ends of the queues. That was when it quietened down, when the shuffling started, when the reason for being was reduced like the sauce in an old cooking pan to the barest extract of what it had previously been. That was when Jay had realised there were queues to join the queues.

The thin tea—no more than hot water with colour—gnawed at the inside of his stomach. He held back from vomiting. He couldn't dispel the recent memory of seeing a woman sick up in the street, and then watching her find two pieces of cardboard to scrape it off the dirty pavement and into a carrier bag. Nothing was left to chance anymore, nothing was wasted. He had known she would fry it for her tea.

He locked the door to his apartment and headed towards the centre of town. Even before the austerity measures had hit the High Street had begun to crumble. The major supermarkets had their suburban outlets and customers fled the traditional shops to bask in what seemed like a utopia of convenience. Places—and names—that Jay had considered staples of life had been boarded up, then replaced by temporary shops with rudimentary signs and badly-spelled window displays. In retrospect they should all have seen it coming. When power is in the hands of the few then there's not much left for the many. And if that power is held high enough, no matter how hard you jump you won't be able to reach it. Jay had held sway in the pubs with these conversations, yet had been shouted down by fools who knew he was right but didn't care about it. He saw one of those fools recently, Gavin his name was, sleeping in a shop doorway, his red hands clinging to a yellow blanket to stave off the cold. In the old days Jay would have lobbed a coin to someone in that state, but now he had to keep his coins to himself. Coins were all that they had.

Where the butcher's used to be, the window was smashed and the replacement 99p store had been looted. It was there that the queue began.

Jay dug his hands in his pockets and joined it.

The queue didn't normally start this far up, but it was a little later in the day and he wondered if he was usually further along the line. Yet when he stuck his head out and followed the queue into the distance he realised that by Scallion Square it split in two. In one direction lay the soup kitchen that he had been heading for, in the other direction was the government shop. The queues usually weren't joined.

A woman in front of him had a blanket over her shoulders and a threadbare 'bag for life' over one arm. Jay considered speaking to her, but no one really did that anymore. People were guarded. Their heads down, their feet shuffled. The camaraderie from moaning about the bad times, or reminiscing about the good old days, had quickly been ground down. It was almost as though you couldn't admit to *be*. And to acknowledge anyone else acknowledged competition for the few items that remained. It was best just to hang in there, until, you had to hope, the tide would turn and reality might begin to reassert itself. Should that ever happen.

Jay glanced left and right. He was less taciturn than the others, yet he felt pressure to be the same. He knew there would be people queuing who didn't know what they were queuing for. For some of them it would simply be something to do, some no doubt did hope for chat. There was a comfort in queuing that Jay couldn't deny. He wondered if it were so orderly in other countries. The television portrayed them as worse than Britain, but he couldn't quite believe it. They had all seen the propaganda before the austerity hit, and even further back they all knew the campaigns that had occurred during the Second World War. Nowadays you couldn't pull the wool over a population's eyes, but you could damn them all the same.

His ears pricked up at the unfamiliar sound of a car engine. As one, the queue turned its head. A green army vehicle curved over the horizon behind them like a beetle. As it reached the end of the queue it slowed and the queue's eyes returned to the ground. Jay, though, kept his head high. The driver looked him square on as he drew level and for a moment there was the shock of recognition without understanding. Then the vehicle pulled to a halt and the driver removed his hat. Jay saw Christopher, one of his old buddies from college.

Something had to be totally fucked up for Christopher to be driving an army vehicle. He had been adamantly anti-government and all the accoutrements which came with it. Quickly, almost unseen, Christopher nodded at Jay. Jay thought for about five seconds with his head and two seconds with his stomach. Leaving the queue behind he found himself climbing into the vehicle beside Christopher. If the queue noticed, they didn't acknowledge it. Within moments Christopher had driven a square through the less visited streets and Jay found himself being taken towards the wood which flanked the town. It was only as they reached the outskirts that Christopher hesitated to speak.

"I know. Say nothing."

Jay held back on his questions. His tongue swelled in his mouth with the anticipation of food. He could only imagine this was why Christopher had picked him up.

They bumped off-road and headed down the barest of tracks towards the lake where Jay had gone fishing as a kid. He'd thought about returning there, but the catch had only ever been sticklebacks and he didn't want to soil his memories by eating such tiny fish. Recent rain had rutted the soil, they rattled over what might as well have been a ploughed field gone hard. After a few moments Christopher pulled up beside a collection of tents. Jay's stomach tensed, not with the thought of food now, but with other fears. The tents, however, appeared to be empty.

"I thought you might be out this way," Christopher said as he switched off the engine. "I couldn't see you leaving like everyone else."

Jay forced words up from his dry throat. "I stuck to my principles."

"No good worrying about those now," Christopher said; then, almost abstractedly, "You hungry?"

He watched as Jay ate the remains of half a tin of Spam. The meat was salty, but it tasted better than Jay could ever remember; or imagine.

"Before all this happened," Christopher said, "I remember reading Spam is a luxury food in South Korea. Something to do with the US army introducing it during the Korean War. They're almost reverent towards it. I laughed when I read it at the time, but I understand it now. I guess you do too."

Jay wiped his mouth with the back of his hand, then licked it. "What happened to you Christopher?"

He shrugged. "I ate more than one tin of Spam, that's all it is. *You* would *now*, wouldn't you?"

Jay wondered if Christopher had something as wild as a cigarette, but the food in his stomach had fired his conscience. Immediately he felt guilty.

"Maybe you should drive me back to the queue."

Christopher shrugged again. "Whatever. Try to help a buddy out." Then he sighed. "This won't last either. Our supplies are no more than yours were a week ago. Won't be long before we're eating each other."

Some thoughts flitted through Jay's head. "What happened to Laura?"

Christopher blinked once, then looked away. It was enough.

"Madeleine got Cotard delusion," said Jay. "You know what that is, right? When all this shit happened she couldn't believe it, wouldn't understand it. The sensation of reality being unpicked unhinged her. She withdrew from me, neglected her personal hygiene and well-being. After a while she began to deny that she existed. She was prone to depression, we both know that—we remember those times at college—but this was different. She would describe herself as a dead body. Then one morning she left."

Christopher looked up. "Where did she go?"

Jay didn't know. But he said: "I imagine she's out there somewhere, with all the rest of them. Queuing."

Christopher picked up a stone and threw it at the side of the vehicle. It left a tiny dent. "You were always one for metaphor."

"When you've got nothing, maybe that's all that's left."

They sat in silence for a moment. Jay knew Christopher would have to drive him back. That the meal had been for old times sake and he could offer nothing more. Yet there was something else there, something Christopher wasn't sure about telling him. Jay knew this, but couldn't prompt it. It would either come or it wouldn't. So he picked up a stick and peeled the bark away whilst he waited. Eventually, Christopher said:

"I've heard things."

"Things? What things?"

"Things that are probably rumour, possibly truth."

"We've all heard rumour: The austerity measures will be over by Christmas. There will *be* a Christmas. The international monetary fund will be re-booted by the banks clearing world debt by wiping it off their spreadsheets. And it'll turn out that on paper they have the same amount of money they have in the vaults and that they did so all along. We've all heard those rumours."

Christopher stood. "I've heard there's somewhere, somewhere close, where none of this is happening."

Jay sighed. "Take me back," he said. "Take me back to the queue."

A few days later when Jay woke, the queue had started much earlier in the morning and was already further back from the High Street than his front door.

He couldn't risk the glow of his portable stove being seen from outside the building so he forwent his usual cup of tea. Instead, he stood and stretched, his bones clicking as though he had rickets; as though he were a wooden animal that hadn't been used for some time.

Jay hadn't seen Christopher since the Spam meal. His last words had been, "We've all got to be going somewhere." He'd even forced out a smile. Jay knew the reference and nodded his head in acknowledgement. It was a nice touch, but otherwise meaningless. The meal he had eaten had falsely indicated to his stomach that more might follow, and in the days which then passed he was hungrier than ever; waking in the night clutched in pain.

Jay left his apartment without bothering to lock it and joined the queue.

It was a misty morning, the sun but a smudge in the sky. He wrapped his arms around himself. Breath hovered at the point of departure from his mouth, and then dissipated to join the haze. The previous evening the television had finally blinked off. That probably explained the length of the queue.

As one, they moved a step forward, then stopped. Jay counted under his breath and it was a full two minutes before they took another step, and by then a dozen new people stood behind him in the queue.

Hours passed. He reached the fork between the soup kitchen and the government stores, between charity and officialdom. For a moment he was held there, as though the two strands of queues were like chopsticks and he were pinched between them. Then he took a step to the left towards the soup kitchen. It wasn't until another twenty minutes had passed before he saw that it also split in two. One strand led to the kitchen and the other headed up Turner Street. Destination unknown.

By the time he reached that choice the pain in his stomach was exploding stars in his head. He dropped to his knees and slumped to the side, but the person behind didn't take his place. They just waited. Slowly, he closed and then opened his eyes; then pushed himself to his knees and then into a sitting position. Finally, he was back on his feet. In another two steps he saw the mural.

He remembered it, of course. It had been there for as long as he could remember. The entire side of an end terraced house had been painted so beautifully that the scene looked real. There was a door, and a ladder to the side of it. At the top of the ladder a man was painting the sky. Another stood with a bucket beside the ladder, looking up. The shadowing was rendered so that it appeared three-dimensional. When Jay first arrived in the town he had in fact believed it was so; it had only been close-up that the subtleties were revealed, the fabrication complete. Today though, there was something different. The door of the painting was ajar.

Jay moved one step further in the queue. It was shadowing, could be nothing else. Either it was always like that and he had never seen it before, or some joker had painted a thin line of black down the unhinged side of the door. But who would have done that? Did such people still exist when all that existed were the queues?

Almost unwillingly, Jay found himself leaving the queue and heading towards the door. The air was still. Mist which had clung to the queue all morning seemed to have evaporated here. He looked back at the queue but could no longer see his place, could no longer remember the back of the person he had stood behind for the past three hours. There was nothing else for it. He reached out and gripped the side of the door.

And it opened.

It was like peeling back a surface layer of the world. As though there were a curtain separating what he knew from what he didn't. The enormity of this reality threatened to overwhelm him, yet he had to keep going. Closing his eyes, he stepped through.

Once he realised he hadn't simply walked into the wall, he opened his eyes.

Everything was different, yet everything was the same.

It was as though the High Street had not been decimated. Everything he remembered was there, filtered by the frequency of light. The view before him was neither transparent nor translucent. It was opaque. His closest approximation was the thin layer of paper which covered photos in an album. If you lifted the paper you saw the photos as they were, yet with the sheen in place the photos were still visible but protected. He had stepped within that protection, yet viewed it as if from outside. For what he saw was protected, yet not quite how it should be.

The streets were empty even if the shops were full. He walked with awe, his hunger not quite forgotten but relegated to a dull ache in his soul. Overhead, birds flew. He saw with a start that they seemed to be following a chem trail, but he couldn't see the plane. Then he returned his gaze to the ground and wandered amongst the places that he knew so well. Although this was a memory he then questioned. Had he come here as a child, and gone fishing in the lake, or had he arrived as a college student and spent all his time in the pub? Cold crept up the back of his spine as if he were suddenly aware of being watched. But when he turned he only saw the back of the building he had walked through. His legs goosebumped all the same.

Closer to the pub he could hear chatter. He rubbed his cheek in puzzlement, then realised he was clean shaven and the beard he had sported for the past few weeks—initially in protest at the austerity measures—was gone. His pockets felt full. Instead of a handful of coins he found his wallet stuffed with notes. Looking up, the occupants of the pub had spilled onto the street. In fact, the shops were busy and cars sped by either side. The further he walked from his entrance point, the more the world was with him.

It was then that he saw her: Madeleine. It was then that she saw him.

Smiles broke out.

She spoke first: "Isn't it wonderful here?"

The words felt wrong. She knew too much. She knew more than he did. There was a knowingness to her expression, a glint in her eye which terrified him.

She pulled him towards the beer garden at the back of the pub where he had often spouted about world affairs when they were no more than abstracts and not harsh realities. On a table, his beer waited; a perfect head. Hers was half-finished.

"I've been waiting for you. I knew you would come, I knew you would find it."

He sat. The seat, the cold sides of the glass, the taste of the beer: all these seemed real enough.

"We shouldn't have been frightened of it," he found her saying. "We should have embraced it all along. The New World Order. Look at it, it's here!"

Jay found himself following her gaze. Through the opacity everything was as it should be, as it *had* been no more than a few months ago. Yet it was still viewed as though beneath a layer. And it was that layer, he realised, that he found unpalatable.

Madeline was talking at her usual speed showing none of the signs of the decline that he had witnessed. Her disintegration of herself as a person had obviously been superseded. But at what cost?

"There are literally hundreds of ancient architectural sites," she said, "such as labyrinths composed of cobblestones in the northern countries, to some of the most audacious town planning here in Britain that you'd never have believed, all based on models of the intestines of sacrificial animals; like the colons of goats. It's incredible, isn't it? Don't you find that incredible? This is one here."

Jay downed half the beer in the hope that it might offer some understanding.

When he looked at Madeline's face it appeared to have been plastered with tracing paper. He could see that thin lines, almost cracks, followed the indentations in her skin.

"There's an entirely new world within this one," she said. "Divined. And when this is gone, there'll be another. And another. Only those of us who have that understanding have been chosen to enter. Don't you see? You won't have to queue here. In here there are no queues."

Jay felt himself shrinking in his own skin, as though there were another one of himself inside who just got smaller, and another in that which got smaller still. The surface was but a façade.

Suddenly he remembered *Disney's* Pinocchio and the promise of Pleasure Island. How everything the boys could ever want was there. And how this desire transformed them into donkeys. Was it too much to imagine that Pinocchio would have become a puppet of the state if he hadn't realised what was happening and tried to escape?

Madeline laughed. *Had he said something funny?* There was almost a bray to it.

Jay was up and running. He tore back along the High Street pushing past pedestrians and weaving in and out of cars; Madeline's laughter in his ears. He burst through the painted door and slewed his way across the queue which appeared to have remained motionless in his absence. But he didn't stop there, he kept on running. He kept on running and running and running in the hope that there would be another door, a further door into a further layer where the austerity didn't exist and never had done. A layer where Christopher had believed none of this was happening. A layer where in fact he was correct, and where fear was something unknown.

He's running still. The queue can see him. That dot on the horizon. If they wait long enough he'll have run around the world.

Things That Are Here Now, Things That Were There Then

Fractured glass sparkles rainbow rays in the sunset, mirrored by surface oil in the puddle where a rusted bicycle is reflected at angles. Rust flakes lift and blow in the wind, thin metallic leaves; pseudo-papery fans which soothe no one. Nearby, crow picks at the ground desultorily. Neither expecting anything nor nothing.

Overhead the wingspan of a plane projects a moving cross on the rough ground, a chemtrail easing from its rear like trailing fish excrement. Once it passes, the shadow is replaced by lengthier ones of approaching evening. To the right of crow, a bud pushes itself up and out of the ground, catches the dying light of the sun, and drinks it in, stores it, anticipating the advent of yet another day. A day which never comes.

Constance always woke with the word *no* in her mouth, a password from dream into awakening. I watched her from the edge of the bed as the sunrise pulled objects from shadows like a magician's reveal. The pine wooden bedroom furniture, the black anglepoise lamp—bent like a tall old man, the hairbrush filled with cement, the television that showed only a film of dust.

If the sun was the magician, Constance was the glamorous assistant. Her natural blond hair fanned across the pillows like fibre optics, her lips a pale smudge on her mouth, her nose a tiny reminder of olfactory memories. She shifted in the bedclothes, reached for me.

I remained quiet. Perhaps she couldn't see me.

Beside her on the bed woke the shadows of the past.

I glanced around the room. Objects which were once here were no longer. Objects which had never been here now were.

Constance had moved with the times. I had moved in.

She blinked. "Did I say it?"

I nodded. "You always say it."

"I saw crow."

"You think you saw crow," I said. "But even in a dream you don't really see."

She rubbed her eyes half-heartedly, resisted awakening. "So you say."

"So I say," I said. Then I reached over and pulled back the bedclothes, revealed nakedness.

Later that morning we exchanged soft kisses tasting of milk. Constance photographed her breakfast both before and after she ate. I took a photograph of her spooning cornflakes into her mouth. She always took more pictures than me.

Outside, shotgun shattered bullets of rain smashed against the windowsill. A summer storm. We had turned off all the electrical items as the skies darkened. Lightning split the clouds like a rip in a dark pillowcase, revealing white feathers. Constance froze for a moment, as if the flash of lightning preceded a photographic shot: as though she posed. To an onlooker, at least, this is what they would have seen. But I saw beyond it. I saw the feathers and the memory.

Constance was an artist, and like all artists her belief in herself was stronger than she was. And this was an integral facet of her artistry because without that belief she would be a checkout girl, an usherette, a baker. Her art came out of herself like sunlight: pure. Yet also erratic. Anything which passed in front of her cast a shadow. And it was in the shadows that the weird stuff was born. The cement filled hairbrush, the upside-down floorboard halfway up the stairs, the childhood photographs with her own face scratched out and then drawn back in. Those elements of Constance represented her dark side, and whilst she didn't know it I was here to cure it.

For eight months she had photographed her every waking task. Finding it insufficient, two months ago she hired me to photograph her in sleep. This proved impossible without falling in love with her, and the romantic artist inside herself realised that it was impossible without falling in love with me.

The difference between us was that her love was a falsehood based on a belief in the purity of art. Whereas mine. Well, mine was also a falsehood, a temporary aberration.

The photographs were all Polaroid's. Constance disliked permanence yet craved it. One copy. This was her compromise. Some of them filled shoeboxes, others Lever Arch files. Those which depicted places within her house were pinned to the walls with interconnected photo clips. We were living inside a house inside a house. Each of the four walls of each of the rooms was wrapped as though from the inside out in photos representing what had been and what no longer was. Imagine, if you will, living inside a memory. Objects changed, but the photographs remained the same.

This was all very well. Until the arrival of crow.

"A crow, you say?"

She shrugged. "What do I know about birds? It's black, has thick wings, a beak, speckles on its feathers like oil on water. I'm not an ornithologist."

"Maybe it's a starling?"

She looked puzzled, a frown creased her brow as though drawing a line under her blond fringe.

"Or simply a blackbird," I ventured.

"No," she said. "It's a crow. And if it isn't, then I want it to be."

Artists always wanted to find significance in everything.

I was the first to tell her that she woke every morning with the word *no* in her mouth.

"Really?" Her eyes were wide, like gobstoppers painted with blue circles.

"Really. It's a reaching out for something. Or, it seems that way."

"Does it worry you?"

I could tell that she wanted it to worry me.

"No, it doesn't worry me," I said. "Has no one told you this before?" I wasn't naïve enough to believe that she had never slept with anyone.

"No," she said. "Maybe it's you."

I thought about that. "Maybe," I said.

That morning she pulled the covers away from me. My foreskin was shrivelled around the head of my penis and she laughed.

"It looks like a walnut whip."

Then she photographed it.

One day she went shopping and I searched for a box of photographs that I knew would exist and which I eventually found under the bed, like a schoolboy's stash of pornography. They were unclear. Body parts captured too close to the skin to identify an owner or owners. I replaced them back carefully and decided not to think about them ever again.

But if Constance had a secret then I also had a secret. I was not who I pretended to be.

Down in the dirt, right at ground level, the twisted spokes of the bicycle spoke volumes about evolution.

Crow alighted on the upended wheel. Its weight shifted the balance. The world turned.

Flowers budded yellow and orange, forcing their way like slo-mo time lapse photography, giving the illusion of speed yet stasis simultaneously. The sun arced across the sky, gave way to night and returned again, repeatedly.

Planes flew backwards across the sky.
A day which repeatedly came, reversed, came again.
If crow could smile, it did.

"What are you studying?"

Constance slipped behind me, one hand snaking around my waist, the other holding her camera.

"Analytical chemistry."

She feigned a yawn, then yawned anyway, setting herself off. "Boring."

"To some, maybe."

She took a photo of my hand on the page. I was lying face down on the carpet in the living room. I say *carpet*, although I was actually lying on photographs of the carpet. Constance reached past me and placed the slowly developing photograph on the floor, stapled it through the carpet and onto the floorboard as the picture of my hand and the book came into focus.

"Read to me," she said.

I shrugged. "It won't interest you."

"It doesn't have to interest me," she said. "Read to me."

So I read: *In analytical chemistry, dark current refers to the constant response produced by a spectrochemical receptor, even in the absence of radiation. Dealing with dark current is a form of blank correction.*

"That *is* boring," she said. She yawned and the flash of the camera captured the inside of her mouth. "What's *blank correction*?"

"Blank correction," I said, "like everything else in the world, is whatever you want it to be."

She moved her snaked-arm away from me. "Blank correction," she repeated. "I like the sound of it."

I closed the book. I understood none of it other than that the seed had to be planted. Dark current was an absence corrected by a blank. A nihilist would have loved it. For Constance, it would be the first step to regaining some sanity.

When I first moved into the apartment, on Constance's insistence, I was bowled over by the sheer amount of photographic evidence of her life. In the bathroom, behind her toothbrush and toothpaste, were several photographs of her toothbrush and toothpaste. The bathroom mirror was almost totally obscured by her reflected face. Within days, mine joined it. The small cupboard under the stairs which she used as a library was like a forest of books. In reality, there were only two shelves; a series of photographs and mirrors turned it into a literary labyrinth. I would reach for a book to find myself reaching for my own hand, in a corner where nothing was real.

"Is this natural?" I asked.

"It is if I want it to be," she said.

"Do you exhibit?"

The answer was coy, revealed nothing: "Doesn't everyone?"

Much later—weeks later—after she had told me her dream of crow—of something she had no control over and could never photograph—I asked: "Do you think he knows about you?"

"Of course!"

I turned on my side, regarded the corner of the bedroom ceiling which was simply a photograph of the corner of the bedroom ceiling. "Do you think he knows about me?"

There was no response. Only another photograph. Myself caught with sleep at the corner of my eye, a gritty memory, the dirt of a dream.

I did some research. To dream of a crow might signify completion of a successful business, but to dream of one flying in cloudy weather denoted anger, loss and misery. Seeing a blackbird meant great trouble, although to hear one sing signified joy and delight. And the starling, well, that was only a small discontent. There was clearly a hierarchy in dream birds. I needed to find out exactly the type of bird, and in doing that there was only one option: to go inside.

Nowhere to hide, nowhere to run.

Never trust a stranger.

Following the advent of crow I bided my time and waited for the right moment. We stayed up late one evening, watching Coen Brothers movies one after the other. She fell asleep, almost unforgivably, during *The Big Lebowski*. After thirty minutes I turned off the DVD, dimmed the lights, then woke her with kisses.

One to the back of her neck, one to her belly, one to her knee, one to the inside of her forearm.

She stirred, woke, the word *no* caught in her mouth and turned to a moan: I had the password. I parted her legs and moved my body across hers, finding no resistance as I eased my way inside her. She invited me in semi-sleep mode, a curling smile on her face, reflected in several of the photographs which adorned the headboard. And then, unlike the other times we had made love, I did something a little different.

I pulled myself onto her, pulled myself against her. Knee bone connected to knee bone, hip bone connected to hip bone, jaw bone connected to jaw bone. Our internal organs touched and merged. I became inside her.

And I sought out the dream.

⊙

Half-concealed in mud, half-congealed in dirt, the metallic shopping trolley stands like a reticent sculpture.

I photo it.

Picking my way across the desolate landscape I capture the images of cans, their metal lids hanging by slivers of tin like robot ballerinas in music boxes. Reddish-brown bricks stand at all angles, lying where they have fallen. Broken glass reflects the light of the flash in this dim setting, a signal to find me should anyone be looking. Crisp packets hold water like bloated frogs. A blue Frisbee, upturned, becomes a bird bath. And it is there that I wait. And sure enough, there's a sound in the air like a thousand feathers falling and after a moment the bird that is black is perched on the rim of the Frisbee, its weight tipping the water towards itself.

It drinks. And behind the oil drum I take a photo.

Constance gasps and I push myself out of the dream and out of her body. The sheets are soaked with blood.

Only the sheets aren't soaked with blood because this is now my dream, and in that dream I wait for the photograph to develop whilst searching through my *Book of British Birds*. Soon, there is a match. I can barely look.

Elsewhere I could have read: *Dark currents within a photosensitive device are reduced through improved implantation of a species during its fabrication.*

No, I don't understand it; but Constance is perfectly correct. As an artist she is completely aware that the world and its meanings can be exactly what anyone wants them to be. And through a positive negation of negative behaviour I can cure her compulsiveness and turn it around.

So I show Constance the photograph and explain that it's a starling and she takes my knowledge as read and she never sees it again.

Sometimes it's as simple as that.

Although crow won't be happy.

There are side effects. She never again says *no* when she wakes.

I know this, although I am no longer there to hear it. Yet *her* knowledge is only imparted in *my* dream.

Before she woke I removed all of the photographs from each and every surface. A blank correction. And in removing the photographs I removed the wallpaper and the bricks and the hidden electricity and the floorboards and the plaster, and each and every item that had ever had any relevance or pseudo-relevance in the life of the artist formerly known as Constance.

She wakes within a white box. A blank canvas. The things that were there then are not there now.

It's what she should have wanted.

And then—because I just cannot resist—I leave a black feather on her pillow: negating the negation.

Within the vestiges of her memory I am the trickster.

Blood For Your Mother

The room smelt of decay. Sunlight bleached through thin, holed curtains, imbuing the room with a warmth which was absent from both of us present. My father's hand lay on top of the bedcovers, stretched towards me with an expectation that I might hold it. But I couldn't bring myself to touch the leathery skin with its bat wing texture; not only from physical disgust, but also because of everything that had so far passed between us.

"I appreciate you coming to see me."

For the moment he was lucid. Yet we had already had this conversation, his dialogue returning like a repetitive child on a fairground ride, or the searching beam of a lighthouse. There were flashes of brilliance, connection, only for these to fade and disappear, before being renewed with equal vigour. By the time this particular goldfish swam around the bowl his memory would be wiped and restored. At times, it was clear that he didn't even know me. At other times I felt he was clutching to a rosy-hued past that existed only for him through the distortion of reminiscence. Either way, like always, our opinions on almost everything were at opposing ends of the spectrum.

"How long has it been?"

I knew it wasn't a question as such, simply another attempt to begin talking. Yet I couldn't hide within internal conversations forever. It was inherent in me to reply.

"I was here yesterday."

"Yes, yes, I know that." *An impatient gateway into his old self.* "You know what I mean."

The words constricted at the end of his sentence, were wheezed out rather than spoken. I remembered an accordion with punctured bellows that I had seen a beggar play in Seville. Ineffectual, ineffective. Those bellows again reminded me of the skin on my father's hands, and as though I was on a roundabout myself I returned to the room.

"Years," I said; "It's been years."

"Years," he repeated and nodded. As though the word were a definite number, satisfying him. "We are both to blame for that."

I could have argued but I didn't have the will.

He attempted to shift himself backwards in the bed, to rise against the slope of the pillow. I remembered his pyjamas which were once a vibrant yellow, now they seemed as faded and decrepit as himself.

"Give me a hand, will you?"

Against my determination I found I couldn't switch off my inherent sense of duty. I stood and reached under his armpits—which to my disgust were damp with sweat—heaving him into a semi-sitting position. In the corner of the room, darkly resembling an executioner's chair, sat a commode which I hoped to God he wouldn't need my help to use.

The feel of his sweat made my hands squirm. I needed an excuse.

"It's been a long journey," I said, although I had spent the night on the sofa and had only travelled the distance of the stairs that morning. "I need to freshen up."

I headed towards the en-suite which was a new addition to the property I knew from my youth, before my father's sudden croak held me back. "No! Not that one. Use the one downstairs."

I hesitated over the door handle, then another wheeze from my father also deflated the defiance in me, and instead I mumbled about being right back and left the bedroom by the usual exit, thumping my way down the creaking stairs and finding myself in the bathroom scrubbing my hands vigorously, rubbing them repeatedly with soap from the dispenser.

I looked at the toilet and then at the wall opposite. When I was a child of a certain height, sitting on the toilet led my gaze to that wall, where, in a whorl combined of too thickly applied paint and indentations in the plaster, I had discerned a face that I sometimes spoke to. A placebo of a God that I knew didn't exist, but which alleviated my complete belief in the unknown that I had always found such a crushing burden. Latterly I came to understand what pareidolia meant, yet even so it remained a comfort. I sat on the toilet, now, and angled my body to child-size, in an attempt to see it again, but either my grown-up stature made it impossible or the re-painting of the bathroom had obliterated its traces. After a while I returned up the stairs, slowly and heavily, to the face that I couldn't avoid.

"I appreciate you coming to see me," my father said.

I decided to leave him to his own devices. It was clear, despite his apparent inability, that he could rise and use the toilet. A neighbour, Mrs Allan, brought him meals in bed. Immediately opposite him a flat-screen television entertained during the day. Whilst he was *in* bed, he wasn't bedridden. There wasn't even the surety that it might be his *death* bed.

I sat in a garden overgrown and choked by weeds; a place where he had once spent many an hour keeping the grass meticulously trimmed with scissors at the borders, and planting shrubs and flowers which would only wither and die at the end of each year. Yet compared to my flat in London, even this wilderness held some beauty. The hint of a segue from Spring into Summer was a pleasant reminder of time spent by the river's edge in the nearby park. Of pooling frogspawn in jam jars, and interlinking daisies in chains. If I closed my eyes I could access the past quite clearly in my memory, as if it were only yesterday.

Yet from time to time a cloud would float by the sun and my demeanour would darken. I would recall the increasing arguments, the constant pre-teenaged sensations of being displaced within the life of my parents, the peeling away of connection with my mother and eventually the desperate banishment imposed on me by my father.

I considered the word *banishment*, which rolled around my head like a metal ball in a bagatelle. But indeed, that was how it felt. I had been edged out of their relationship, as though my birth had imposed on them rather than been a blessing. I couldn't put my finger on how or when that had happened, but the resentment was there; and upon my departure for university I couldn't but help to hear the delight of their plaudits as a cleansing wind of relief that swept through the house and blew me out of there for good.

And once out, it was all too easy to keep myself busy, to forge a career, to return only for anniversaries and Christmases, and even then to find my presence an accepted necessity rather than a true welcoming. Whilst this might possibly have been expected from my father, who was always preoccupied and distant, the mental pushing away I had felt from my mother hurt the most. As though it was done against her will, yet was done all the same.

"You sit there too long you'll take root."

I opened my eyes to see Mrs Allan standing with the sun behind her. Seeing me squint she then moved and her shadow fell across my face, and as she slipped from light into dark her features reformed like a developing negative.

"It's a shame about the garden," she continued, as though I had spoken. "But I can't do everything."

I liked Mrs Allan. She had been my parents' neighbour for as long as I had been born. Her husband had worked in the Rowntree Mackintosh chocolate factory which had subsequently closed down. The eggs I had received at Easter always came from there.

"He's in a bad way, isn't he?" I said. "He needs help."

"He won't accept it from anyone other than me. And I'm getting old myself." She smiled a smile that belied her years, was still filled with pre-middle-aged hope.

"I know you do all you can," I said. "But he needs Social Services. A carer could help him get up and dressed. He shouldn't remain in bed, he'll get sores. He needs an occupational therapy assessment for grab rails and possible adaptations. God knows how he uses the stairs."

Mrs Allan's sympathy rolled off her like waves on untouched sand. "I don't think he goes downstairs," she said. "Everything he has is upstairs."

"Even so..." But I let the words hang. I was wary of suggesting that the help Mrs Allan gave wasn't enough, although at the same time I could predict my embroilment in my father's remaining years like the realisation a mastodon might have had when sinking into the La Brea tar pit. I didn't want to be his main carer. I wasn't even sure why I was there.

"Well," Mrs Allan said, as though in summary of all we had discussed. She turned and headed for the back door. "I'll get this up to him whilst it remains hot. But maybe you could give social services a call. It wouldn't hurt for him to acknowledge his condition."

I closed my eyes and thought over her words. She knew more than anybody how my mother's death had affected my father. And she was right, he couldn't be allowed to wallow in self-pity until the remainder of his days; despite the resentment I felt towards him I couldn't allow that to happen. Yet even as I thought it I knew I was simply intent on shifting the burden onto someone else, someone professional who would have no emotional involvement and who could concentrate solely on what was necessary.

"We need to talk," my father said. He stood by the window, peering through the curtains at the sunset which placed the garden in sharp relief, the light making it clear that my attempts to tame the vegetation that day were no more than a bad haircut.

I wanted to say that conversation between us died many years ago, that I couldn't formulate words as an adult that fit with the child I believed he expected me to be, that—quite simply, horribly—I had nothing to say to him. But instead I said, "What do you want to know?"

I hoped he would ask me questions about my work as a radiographer, about the two long-term relationships I'd had which eventually came to naught, about my fight with breast cancer and my narrow escape from a mastectomy, about how or where I was living, or the contrast between London and here, but instead I knew he was talking about himself, about laying ghosts to rest.

"I loved your mother. That much was clear, wasn't it?"

"You loved each other," I said, fighting to keep the bitterness out of my voice.

He saw none of it. "If you understand that then you understand how it needed to be."

He turned away from the window. Those yellow pyjamas hung loose on his body like flesh, giving him an almost translucent appearance as the sun blinked below the horizon. "Help me back to bed, would you."

I touched his elbow and guided him, but there was no greater physical contact than might be used to bob a balloon in one direction over another.

He sat on the edge of the bed and looked at me, before swinging his own legs up and under the covers. On the bedside cabinet the remains of Mrs Allan's cottage pie were congealed in a circle around the rim. I had a sudden, repulsive, desire to taste it.

"There's so much I need to tell you, so much you need to understand."

This might be either of us speaking, yet it was him.

"I'm drained," he said, eventually. "I can't go on anymore."

"You need some help," I voiced. "I can't stay longer than a week. My job..." yet my words fell away, sounding like the poor excuses they were.

In other cultures they have large families so that old age can be accommodated as part of life, with everyone mixing in, taking their turns, alleviating the burden which they don't even see as a burden. But here, and especially with me as a single child—a disenfranchised single child—it was different. Even if I loved him I knew I would want to be out of there. I didn't want to partake in the rituals or the dance of death; particularly if that dance were to be a long one.

He nodded, though, with understanding. "You youngsters."

He knew I was fifty-six. I know I felt it.

Perhaps it was because of this that I felt a sudden urge for the truth, for closure before the possibility was closed.

"I just want the truth, dad."

"You're not ready for it."

"Then why am I here. Why did you call for me?"

"She needs you." Again, that wheeze. "Can't cope alone."

I was about to ask for clarification, but suddenly he slipped and I realised to my annoyance he had fallen asleep. He must have been weaker than I thought.

So Mrs Allan can't keep you going, I thought. *So my request to be here came from her rather than you.* Of course, I suspected that when Mrs Allan had managed to track me down, but it hurt to hear the words. My father only needed me because the neighbour couldn't keep him alive. It resolved my decision to call social services the following morning.

Even so, before I flicked off the light and left the room, I found myself popping his arm under the blanket and ensuring his body was fully covered. There are some instincts which are innate and cannot be avoided.

Downstairs I flitted between the kitchen and living room. The blankets I had used whilst I slept on the sofa the previous evening were half-turned onto the floor, as though I had been a snake sloughing skin. Not for the first time I considered why I hadn't spent the night in my old room, why I hadn't even peeked inside it. Now I knew that I avoided it in case it evoked fond memories and pushed against my assertion that I had rarely been happy here.

Suddenly, I burst into tears.

I needed an out. Grabbing my coat and checking that the key Mrs Allan had provided for me was in the pocket, I headed to the front door, rubbing my eyes with the back of my hand. I was just about to leave when I heard a noise upstairs resembling a gigantic sigh, as if the house itself were exhaling. I paused, my heart hammering, waiting to hear it again, but after a minute, possibly two, of complete and utter silence, I decided there was no concern and I let myself out and into the night.

It was still warm, yet I had been sensible to wear the coat. *Sensible* was a word which sat awkward with me, something I had flirted with my whole life, been attracted to and repelled by; a word I equated with stability. Yet I had none of it really, or rather I had traded stability with excitement, leaving my life boring and nondescript and dissatisfied. Or maybe unrecognised.

I glanced at my watch. It was approaching eleven o'clock. Shortly the villagers would be dispersed from the *Dog 'n' Duck* and they would return to their homes, some more directly than others. I decided to head for the park and subsequently the river. My memory would be my light. I knew the direction intimately. Even so, Mrs Allan had warned me of the council's new part-time streetlighting policy which would mean all artificial light would be extinguished after midnight. It only occurred to me now that she realised I would need to walk.

The river ran through the village, with footways that criss-crossed it picturesquely over white-wooden humped bridges. These surfaces were slick with duck excrement, and though it was dark an occasional quack confirmed their existence. I let my feet fall into familiar patterns, as though literally walking in the footsteps of my younger self, and as I did so memories resurfaced like flotsam and jetsam, unbidden yet welcome, painful yet happy.

I took each one, folded it carefully, and replaced it in the cupboard of my mind.

It had been my father who had told me that not only had my mother died but she was already buried.

"I couldn't contact you," he had said, the conversation itself belying the authenticity.

I remember slumping against the fridge, then forcing myself to sit in a chair, the cord from the wall-mounted phone stretched in a tangent that raised my elbow to an uncomfortable position.

He answered my questions. She had become obese, of this I had known. Diabetes had set in. There was either an iron deficiency or surplus, I don't remember which. There had been blood transfusions. Lots of them. He had to spell *transfusional hemosiderosis* and I had to look it up. But in reality none of this mattered, the whys and wherefores. What mattered was that my mother had died without the opportunity of speaking to me. What mattered was that even though she hadn't been there in my life for some time, now she was no longer *there* to be there.

I remember replacing the handset shaking with anger; my emotions a whirligig. My father hadn't tried hard enough to contact me. He hadn't even tried.

In the dark, the park seemed larger than it was. In one corner, outlines of children's play equipment kept stark relief in the moonlight. I resisted the urge to sit on a swing. It wasn't my swing anyhow, this wasn't my park. The towering metal slides had been replaced with twentyfirst century user-friendly equipment, the concrete floor mutated into woodchip and then into something disconcertingly spongy. Instead I skirted the play area and followed the sound of the river which went underground in the centre of the village and emerged at the rear of the park. It was, in theory, possible to follow it around its course until it reached the next village—a journey I had made many a time—but I knew I wouldn't be so foolhardy at night.

All I wanted was to sit and listen to its babble. To close my eyes, feel the dark press around me with the lightest of touches, and to connect—however briefly—with the past future and the universe under the openness of the sky. To find some peace amongst the hubbub of conflicting thoughts that inhabited my mind.

The grass was damp. I did my thinking. Mrs Allan was right, when I returned to the village there wasn't a streetlight in operation. It felt to me like I had closed them all down.

"You're through to Roxy on the social care line, can I take a note of your name please?"

"Miriam Hubbard."

"And how can I help you today, Miriam?"

I made ink doodles on a junk mail envelope as Roxy told me there was no access to social services without my father's consent. That without that consent there could be no assessment. That if he chose to spend the rest of his days uncared for then that was his unequivocal right. That if I believed he had the onset of dementia it was a matter for his GP. That if there was anything else they could help me with then I should naturally give them a call.

I could clearly see a trapdoor opening under my feet, with vociferous demons ready to swallow me whole should I take on the role of carer, or alternatively, to condemn Mrs Allan to the same fate. Mrs Allan, who was in her early eighties herself, who was also standing over a trapdoor that was starting to creak beneath the weight of her years.

I held my head in my hands. Whilst my father had made no direct request for me to remain there as carer, I knew I had to convince him against it. I wasn't the person to cope. He needed outside help.

Upstairs I knocked and waited, unwilling to disturb him on the commode.

He put down a book as I entered. Jean Paul Sartre's *Iron In The Soul.* I was about to say, *Since when did you become an existentialist*, but instead I said "Don't say it."

"Don't say what?"

"That you appreciate me coming to see you."

He shrugged. "Why would I say that? You've been here two days already."

I couldn't help muscles forcing the usually downturned corners of my mouth into the hint of a smile. "Are you feeling better?"

He nodded. Yet there was a tiredness around his eyes, and he seemed to have lost even more weight than yesterday. Despite the cottage pie.

"You need some help here," I launched. "Mrs Allan can't go on forever, and I have to return to London. This isn't my place anymore."

He opened his mouth. Closed it. Opened it again. "There's no one else who might take over."

"Take over?"

He sighed. "I'm dying."

I knew it, had known it, but his words fell from his mouth like a slab of meat onto a butcher's counter.

"It's not for me that I asked you to come."

A shiver of uncertainty ran through me. Did this apparent lucidity hide madness? Did I prefer him incoherent?

"Listen," I began, but he interrupted me.

"No. You listen. Miriam, have you ever been pregnant?"

The question felled me. "What? I...No, no; I haven't been. What is this?"

Words tumbled out of him, suddenly, a release of pent frustration. "Then you wouldn't understand the cravings. The cravings women have when they are pregnant. The cravings your mother had with you."

I shook my head. "I don't understand. I don't see how this is relevant."

"Blood."

"Blood?"

"Your mother craved blood when she was pregnant. Others crave ice-cream, pickled cucumbers, even coal, but your mother craved blood."

I almost laughed, despite my confusion. "You're saying she was some kind of vampire."

He shook his head. There was effort in the motion. "She was no kind of vampire. That's the stuff of films and nonsense. She was some kind of else."

"Some kind of nonsense!"

A wheeze. "You have no idea how much it hurt us to not have you here." His hand twitched on the bedcover. He wanted a physical touch that I wasn't prepared to give. "But you couldn't be. You would have seen."

I stood. "I would have seen what? That neither of you wanted me, that you detested the fact that I was born, that somehow I spoiled your lives and you couldn't wait to get rid of me?" I had raised my voice before I knew it. "Perhaps it would have been best for *you* to have died before my arrival. Maybe I could have missed your funeral too." I headed for the door, tears sparkling my eyes, a heaviness around my heart that restricted my breathing. I had no idea what do to or where to go. But I needed out. I needed out.

Another wheeze, of extreme effort, as though a hurricane forced through a straw. "Miriam. Your mother isn't dead. She's in the next room."

I stopped. Closed my eyes. All the weight of the years fell away from me as though the house were falling apart, a demolishment of everything I took for granted.

"What?"

"It's true." He fell back into the bed as I turned. I realised he had been outstretched towards my departing figure. "She's there. She needs you."

Another wheeze and his eyes closed. I bent over him cautiously. He was still breathing. It was exhaustion that had extinguished him, but it was only temporary. I gave a little laugh, forcing hysteria out of it. The only logic was to dispel fantasy completely. I needed to restore order to my life.

Opening the door to the en-suite bathroom I walked in and saw my mother.

If I hadn't been told it was her then I wouldn't have known. She was unrecognisable. She wasn't recognisably human.

I took in everything at once, disbelieved it immediately, and then slowly forced myself to believe it.

My eye had been caught by a plastic bag of blood hung by the door, feeding a drip that ran into flesh packed into the room from floor to ceiling. This was no en-suite, it was a purpose-built container. It confined what was inside.

Flesh stretched taut like a frog's air sac was my mother's naked belly, distended completely out of proportion to the rest of her form. Within the belly, the skin was sufficiently translucent to see red swirling patterns of corpuscular liquid. I vomited quickly onto the floor, over my shoes. Her arms and legs barely supported her, resembled elephantine tree trunks on the island of Socotra. Pushed into the top right hand corner of the room, against the grey painted walls and ceiling, her face gurned at me. I let out a scream and quickly closed the door, yet not before I saw the absolute sadness and desperation that floated in her eyes.

I sat on the bed, awash with sickened wonderment, oblivious to my father behind me.

I can only describe it as a dream.

I passed Mrs Allan on the stairs, the smell of home-cooked lasagne trying to stimulate my stomach to hunger despite everything I had seen. The push of nature against disbelief. The reminder that *things go on*.

Outside, the fresh air did little to shake me out of reverie. I found myself walking around the village, glancing at headlines on the newspapers that rippled in a breeze outside the newsagents, exchanging a handful of nods and comments with people who knew me and hadn't seen me for years. Normality pressed around me from all sides, tried to imprint itself on my consciousness, restore my sanity, but none of it could dispel what I knew I had seen.

The reality of my father's situation was ever more present. Under no circumstances could a carer from social services meet his needs. Nor could a doctor be allowed to discover the reason for his apparent weakness, his no doubt extreme and repeated loss of blood. Yet nothing had changed from yesterday. I still did not want that role. The fact was I remained abandoned. For whatever reason, their life was one that I didn't want to lead.

I had to act before I could assimilate my knowledge, before I started to reason with myself, before I could fully believe that nightmare and truth were one. Because of this, I found myself returning to the home much quicker than I had imagined. In fact, Mrs Allan was only just leaving as I arrived.

"He seems a little perkier today," she said with a smile. "Wolfed down that lasagne."

"Do you know?"

"Do I know what?"

"Nevermind."

In the kitchen I opened a packet of Lincoln biscuits, but they were old. The taste dry in my mouth. I spat them out. Then regarded the mess I had made on the linoleum and once again found myself suppressing a laugh.

When I sighed I found the physical process sharp in my mind. It was clear that breathing was a process of inflating and deflating. Of stopping and beginning again. There was no question of what I had to do.

I went out into the garden that I had ineffectually cleared the previous day and picked up the fork that leant beside the shed. Every movement I took seemed fantastical, other-worldly.

At the top of the stairs I hesitated outside my father's room. Then I turned right and went into that *other* room. The one that contained all my young memories. My bedroom.

When I realised it was how I left it I understood it was their shrine. I closed the door behind me and was one, two, four, eight, sixteen again.

I sat on my bed and waited until dark; thought I could hear breathing through the walls. Through the open curtains the streetlights sharpened the tines on the fork. Made them more real. None of this would be easy, but then none of life had been easy. I knew afterwards I would sit beside my father on his bed and wonder in silence whether I might hold a pillow over his face or let him continue living with grief. As I considered this, night fell deeper. Outside—under the burgeoning sky—it seemed darker than dark. The moon was obscured by clouds.

When my mother burst, the room was shocked red; like a mosquito squashed under a thumb.

www.ingramcontent.com/pod-product-compliance
Lightning Source LLC
Chambersburg PA
CBHW030545310726
48979CB00010B/2033/J
* 9 7 8 1 9 0 8 1 2 5 4 5 3 *